Love Imperfect

L. Lee Shaw

Boho Books

Love Imperfect

Boho Books, 36179 S. Sawtell Road, Molalla, OR 97038

ISBN: 978-0-9988455-2-4 (paperback)

978-0-9988455-3-1 (ebook)

Cover Photos: Shutterstock

Printed in the United States of America

Boho Books paperback edition 2018/ Revised 2021

Love Imperfect

Jon Imperfect

Contents

Chapter 1

Colton Williams nosed his battered Ford Ranger pickup truck into an empty slot beside a box van emblazoned with bags of potato chips on the sides. It wasn't technically a parking space, but New Year's Eve had the convenience store parking lot filled to overflow. Heading to the doors, he could see a line of people snaking around by the coolers on the back wall over the half painted windows. The majority were carrying beer and wine in anticipation of the night's celebrations.

He held the door for a couple of exiting customers before slipping inside. Even though his mother was busy ringing up purchases, she spotted him waiting beside the ATM machine to the right of the door.

"She's in the store room changing. I'm sure she won't mind if you go in," she said with a wink.

Colton worked his way around to a door in the back. Pulling it open, he stepped inside. There was a short hall leading to a couple of swinging metal doors. He pushed open one of the doors. His mother was right. Tiffany's clothes were draped over a box. However, he had a hard time seeing her under a man dressed only in a striped shirt with the same logo as on the van he parked next to.

He gave the door a hard shove and let it go. The whuppety sound of it swinging followed him back into the store. He ignored his mother calling after him as he pushed out into the cold night. In a moment, she saw his pickup back up and swing out of the parking lot.

At home, Colton got a beer from the refrigerator before retreating to his bedroom. His Siamese cat, Cinnamon, stretched languorously on his pillows as he sat down on the bed and took a long swallow from the bottle.

1

His cell phone vibrated in his pocket. He pulled it out. Yeah, it was Tiffany.

"What?" His voice was harsh.

"Hey, handsome, I'm waiting." She was using her sultry voice.

"I was there but you were pretty occupied with Mr. Chips." He heard a sharp inhalation on her end. "That told me all I need to know about our relationship. We don't have one." He disconnected. His phone rang almost immediately. It was her again. He punched her number, disconnected, and then blocked it. For Colton, over meant over.

He sprawled, working his way up to lean back against the headboard supported by his pillows, shifting the cat to his stomach. As Colton stroked her, he recognized he wasn't particularly upset or angry. He was, in fact, relieved Tiffany set the stage so he could exit. It was like there was more air around him. Tiffany had always been hyper-possessive. She'd phone him dozens of times during the day when she knew he was working and couldn't talk to her. If he held the door for some elderly lady she would accuse him of wanting to cheat. Their time together had been nonstop drama.

Cinnamon peeled off of him when his mother threw the door open. "So what the hell is going on? Tiffany was in hysterics when I left the store. She says you stood her up and now you won't talk to her. Since I know you were there, you want to tell me why you took off without her?"

"First of all, Mom, would you knock before busting in here. I could have been changing or something."

"I've seen you naked. You were born that way."

"And that was a long time ago. Secondly, when I went to get Tiffany, she was busy servicing the potato chip guy. I didn't want to interrupt so I left—permanently."

His mom studied him for a moment. "So I guess that means you're back on the market. A couple of the other girls will be glad to hear that."

"Why don't you let me handle my own life? I'll decide when I'm 'back on the market'."

"Sure, you've done a great job of handling it so far," she said as she banged his door closed.

Colton stared at his TV's darkened screen, feeling emotionally letdown. He realized his youthful fantasy of finding and falling in love with someone special had burned out in the stream of Tiffanys and her ilk where it was all drama, possessiveness, and, if it lasted more than a few months, the push for marriage. Apparently special didn't exist anymore; probably it never had.

Regardless, he was through investing anymore of himself in relationships where the other person always thought it was just about her. Maybe his mom was right. Love was just another way for life to kick you in the teeth. No reason to waste any more time looking for something which always ended up exactly that way.

*****

Although spring was officially just a week away, the coming season was not yet recognizable as the leaden skies of the Oregon winter remained constant. Colton wondered if the chill late afternoon drizzle made the old neighborhood he drove into feel more decayed than it might have been. Turning at the corner and parking, he picked up a clipboard from the passenger seat, double-checking to see if he was at the right location before getting out of his truck.

Colton flipped up the collar of his jean jacket against the dripping sky as he walked around to the front of the house. Although bedraggled curtains still hung in the front window, there were no lights or other signs of habitation. He gingerly climbed the front steps, avoiding the obviously rotted places. Colton peered in the narrow windows on either side of the door, but the dull day and dark house allowed little from being seen.

Turning to glance around, he noted the house across the street was bright with lights including a sign that said open. After carefully stepping back down the stairs, he sprinted across the street as the drizzle briefly intensified. A sign hanging from the covered porch identified the location as Tin Roof Gallery.

Outside the door, he stripped out of his jacket and gave it a good shake before slipping it back on. When he turned the glass doorknob and pushed, a faint tinkling sound could be heard. Almost instantly, a warm voice called, "Be right there."

Soft jazz played as he heard footsteps crossing the upstairs floor before coming down the stairs. The first thing he saw was a pair of tan knee-high boots over slim jeans. The front tails of a faded denim shirt were tucked in and arms extending out of an oversized rust colored jacket were filled with large balls of yarn; one of which fell and rolled in his direction leaving a long trail of green in its wake.

He bent to grab it as it approached his feet. When he stood up, he looked into a pair of the bluest eyes he had ever seen. They were the clear blue of a summer sky. It felt as though sunlight shimmered across them. As she turned to dump the rest of the yarn on the counter by the door, his attention moved to the thick bundle of hair staked to the top of her head by two chopsticks.

She reached for the yarn with one hand while holding out her other. "Hi, I'm Mya," she said. An enchanting dimple formed near her mouth when she smiled.

Something about her slammed into his midsection and it took a moment for him to react coherently. He let go of the yarn, transferring his clip board to the vacated hand as he shook her hand. "I'm Colton Williams," he said.

She tilted her head, looking at him questioningly. "So, how can I help you?"

Under the gaze of those eyes, he fumbled mentally. Shifting the clipboard back, he grabbed his focus and motioned to the house across the street.

"I was wondering if you had any information about what was going on with the place over there," he said pointing.

She looked out the window. "Mr. Gillespie's house? He was moved to a nursing home in the fall. Mr. Stavros down the street told me he passed away around Christmas. I think he had a son in California. Why? Are you interested in buying it?"

Colton shook his head. "No. I work for a construction company that also occasionally invests in derelict houses, renovates them, and then resells. I check out properties for them."

Inexplicably, like a cloud scudding across the sun, her face darkened for a moment. It passed and her smile brightened again.

Colton glanced around, seeking an excuse to linger. He gestured to the work hanging in the main room. "Who does all this?" he asked.

"I do. Or most of it." She moved to a pedestal with a smallish clay box covered over with symbols perched on it. "My friend, Nancy, does the ossuary boxes."

"Ossuary boxes?"

"Yes. It was an ancient way of burying a person's bones."

He involuntarily stepped back. "Okay, that's creepy."

She laughed. "Nancy is a counselor and uses them in her practice to help people bury the past. They're so cool, though, I begged her to let me display some here."

Turning his back on the boxes, he began to circle the room, carefully looking over the collection. "You do all this?"

Remaining beside the pedestal, she answered. "Yes, the paintings, quilts, and weavings are mine."

He stopped in front of a small weaving hanging from what looked like driftwood. The undulating blue in it reminded him of her eyes. Glancing at the price card next to it, he was surprised by the number on it; one hundred dollars for something maybe four inches by six inches.

Returning to the entry area, he unconsciously set his clipboard on the counter as he leaned over to look at a large metal ring clamped onto an art easel. "What's this?"

"It's a work in progress. I'm trying to emulate a spider's web from the spider's point of view. Not very successfully at the moment."

"Spider?"

"Yes. Have you ever stopped and watched one spin its web? They are amazing artists, although a little redundant. Each spider weaves only one pattern of web its whole life, but each web is as individual as our fingerprints."

He glanced down at her. She was eyeing her project thoughtfully.

"You study spiders and their webs?"

A mischievous twinkle came into her eyes as she looked at him. "Doesn't everyone?"

He slowly shook his head. "No. Most people are grabbing for the nearest thing to smash them."

A small alarm began to beep. She reached over the counter to pull out her cell phone and push an icon. "Tin Roof Gallery is now closing for the day."

He was reluctant to leave. "Isn't there a tavern nearby?"

"The Sellah is just a block over."

"This may be out of line, and please tell me if it is, but would you let me buy you a beer for your help today and your time?"

She looked at him appraisingly for moment. "Give me a moment."

Circling around the counter, she pulled out a canvas carryall and swept the yarn into it before moving the easel to the corner by the window, storing the bag under it. She then trotted up the stairs.

As he waited, he looked around. He recognized the whole space had been remodeled and updated; every inch of walls and ceilings painted a clear bright white. The floor looked original, with the wood planks stained a pale grey. One or more rooms had been opened to create the large exhibition space to the left of the centrally placed stairwell. He could see a kitchen area through a door off the open area on the right side of the stairs and another door had a small painted sign stating it was the restroom. Except for the counter, the remaining largish space was bare.

Mya was zipping a vintage leather bomber jacket as she came downstairs. At the foot of the stairs, she loosely wrapped a long scarf around her neck. Her hair was hidden in a dark red slouch beanie.

She flicked off the open sign and turned the dimmer switch by the front door, lowering the lights throughout the first floor.

Day had disappeared into dusk when Colton opened the front door. She locked it after he pulled the door shut. "My truck is just across the street," he said as they descended the stairs.

"It would take you longer to circle back than it will for us to walk over," she said as she turned left toward the corner of the block. Once they reached the corner, she turned left again.

Looking around, Colton noted a number of the houses were dark with overgrown vegetation, deepening the shadows around them. He glanced at Mya. She didn't seem bothered by her surroundings. "It looks like a lot of places are empty," he commented.

"Yes. Many of the older people have passed or been moved out of places they lived much of their adult lives. The houses look so sad. It's like they are waiting for their former owners to come back and make them right again."

It was such an unexpected take on the neighborhood he turned his head in her direction just as her boot heel slid on the soggy moss creeping across the sidewalk.

He grabbed for her arm as she lost her balance. As she regained her footing, he tucked her hand under his arm. "I think maybe you should hang on."

She tried to pull her hand back. "Thanks, but it's not like I don't know about the killer moss stalking this neighborhood. I just wasn't paying attention."

He placed his hand over hers, firmly keeping it in place, as they resumed walking.

Although his expression had been protective, not predatory, she was careful to maintain space between his body and hers. She did not want to send the wrong message. She totally was not into one-night stands or casual couplings. And she really did not want to resort to the pepper spray tucked in her pocket.

Reaching the curb opposite their destination, Colton whistled softly through his teeth. "Okay, that's different," he said as he eyed the tavern dug into a low hillside while one of the large old houses common to the area squatted over it.

The inside proved just as eccentric with unmatched old tables scattered over the colored concrete floor; each surrounded by equally mismatched chairs. The bartender was tall and lanky, his kinky red hair pulled up in a man bun creating an odd balance to the red beard covering the lower part of his face.

A young woman was leaning against the bar. She straightened up when they entered. Her platinum bleached hair spiked out around a face dotted with nose, eyebrow, and lip piercings. The tee-shirt under her moto jacket strained over her ample bust; the material slashed to play peek-a-boo with the unrestrained voluptuousness. Black leggings stopped short of the top of her combat boots.

Mya led the way to a table towards the back. Raising her voice slightly, "Since some people, ahem, Jacob, are so cheap about heating this place, you have to sit back here to keep from freezing."

The man at the bar bounced back a rejoinder. "And if some people would drink more, I might be able to afford to turn on the heat."

Colton pulled out a chair for Mya, carefully slipping it under her as she sat. He took the chair opposite her. The girl from the bar clumped up to the table and placed a glass in front of Mya before turning, what she considered her ample charms, on Colton.

7

"And what can I get you," she asked as she jostled her arms to draw attention to her assets. Mya watched with amusement as Colton glanced quickly at and then away from Nyla's chest.

"Hefeweizen, please."

Mya tilted her head slightly as she focused on Colton's face. His dark brown eyes were almost identical in color to his hair. There was a scruffy sexiness in the couple of day's growth of beard surrounding a mouth that ....

"Down, girl," she thought as she unzipped her jacket; slipping her arms out of it and letting it fall over the back of her chair.

"What is that you have?" Colton asked, gesturing toward her glass.

Jacob loomed over them as he put Colton's beer in front of him. "A beer slushy. An exclusive creation for someone who can nurse one single beer all night. You, sir, have hit the jackpot. Mya is a budget date if ever there was one. And perhaps you know this, but just in case, don't let her talk you into a game of pool. It will not end well. You have been warned."

Colton looked at her. "That good, huh?"

She answered with a shrug as she took a tiny sip of her beer ice. "So what else do you do besides look at properties for your employer?"

He lifted an eyebrow quizzically.

She reached across the table to take one of his hands. Turning it over, she lightly ran her fingers across the callouses. "These are working man hands; not a desk jockey's."

The smile hovering at the corner of his mouth disappeared. "I do construction. But my employer pays extra for checking out properties for possible purchase. It's a way of bringing in some bucks during the slow times." There was an edge in his tone.

"I totally get that," she replied. "I paint store windows with artwork to supplement my commissions. I do as many as I can during the holidays and seasonal changes to build up my stash of cash for my slow months."

"So how did you end up with your gallery in this neighborhood? It's kinda a long ways from where the trendy kids hang out."

"It's what I could afford. The house was totally decayed when I bought it. It took me and my friends almost two years to tear it apart and put it back together."

He reached across and turned her hand over. "These do not look like working man hands."

"Oh, trust me; they definitely have done their share of swinging a hammer and running a power saw, not to mention power drills, sanders and paintbrushes. Plus, for a while, I could give you the location of every construction dumpster in the city."

"Construction dumpsters?"

She nodded. "Do you have any idea how much great stuff construction crews throw away? Sorry, that was dumb. Of course, you do. Anyway, we scavenged them almost every day. I got permission from each job site to take whatever was tossed in the dumpster. It's how I found all the beadboard I used in the ceilings and upstairs. When I stopped to ask permission to dumpster dive at a new place, I spotted one of the workers bringing out a section. They were setting them aside so I asked if they might be selling them and, if so, how much. The guy I talked to said he would find out and let me know if I came back the next day."

She paused as Nyla came up to the table and pointed to Colton's almost empty glass. He nodded, swallowed the remainder, and handed it to her. Mya waited until another had been set in front of him.

"Anyway, I went back the next day and all of the beadboard was lying on top in the dumpster. The guy I had talked to the day before stuck his head out of the door and hollered, 'You want to haul it, it's yours'."

He wondered if she understood just how far a pair of startlingly beautiful blue eyes and a mouth just begging to be kissed could go in getting what she wanted.

"Are you still into dumpster diving?"

A lovely flush stained her cheeks. "I've reformed. I'm more into picking up free things off of curbs and flea markets now."

"So where do you live, I mean when you're not at the gallery?"

"I actually live at the gallery. It has everything I need... kitchen, bedroom, bath. How about you?"

"I live over on Washburn."

She recognized the area; little homes once built as low-income housing, now part of some kind of urban renewal project "Apartment?"

He shook his head; his expression was both slightly defensive and embarrassed. "No. My mom and I share a little house. She works hard, but she still can't quite manage the mortgage on her own."

"I take it your dad isn't around."

Colton's face darkened. "No. He's dead."

"I'm sorry."

A spark flashed in his eyes. "Don't be."

The conversation was veering in places he did not want to go when they were just getting acquainted so he gestured to the pool table. "How about showing me your chops?"

Her look was impish. "Okay. But to be fair, I'll let you break first."

They racked up the balls at the table and Colton leaned over to shoot. He ran two balls and then missed the third shot.

Mya slowly chalked her cue as she studied the lay of the table. She circled the table, set up her shot, and then ran the rest of the balls.

"Well, I did sink two of them," Colton said with a smile.

"Rack them up and I will break," Mya answered. When the last ball dropped into the pocket without him being able to take a shot, he came and gently pulled the cue out of her hand. "I think we're done. I can only stand so much public humiliation in a single evening. Besides, I need to pick up my mom from work. Her car is in the shop until tomorrow. And just how did you get so freakin' good?"

She just smiled as she retrieved her jacket off the back of the chair. He took it and held it out so she could slip her arms in the sleeves.

The walk back to the gallery was quiet. At the walkway leading to her porch, she turned and held her hand out. "Thank you, Colton. It was nice meeting you."

He shook his head. "I'm sorry, but a gentleman escorts a lady to her door."

At the door, she again held out her hand. Ignoring it, he reached up to her beanie. Slipping it off, he watched as her golden brown hair cascaded over her shoulder, rippling down before ending at her hip. "I've wanted to do that all evening."

He then took the key she had pulled out of her pocket and unlocked her door, opening it slightly. Colton sensed Mya stiffening.

He responded by handing her back the key with only a brush of his hand against hers.

Without saying anything else, he made his way down the stairs; crossing to his truck. He looked in the rearview mirror as he put the key in the ignition and turned over the engine. Mya was on the porch waving something in his direction. The clipboard he had forgotten on the counter. Smiling to himself, he put the truck in gear and pulled away from the curb. Now he had a real reason to come back.

Chapter 2

In the convenience store parking lot, he pulled into a spot as close to the door as he could find since the earlier drizzle was now flat out rain. Getting out, he dashed to the overhanging entry way of Deuce's Express. His mom was leaning against the wall clutching a plastic bag.

She waved it in his direction as soon as she saw him. "Chimi-changas and poppers," she called as she straightened up. Handing him the bag, she slung her purse over her shoulder and both raced back to the truck.

Pulling the truck onto the two strips of concrete serving as the drive way, Colton jumped out and headed to the door. Unlocking it, he switched on the porch light and motioned for his mother.

As soon as she stepped out of the truck, an ungodly screaming was heard through the open door. "Geez, Cinnamon, we just got home," Colton said.

"And whose idea was it to get a Siamese cat in the first place?" his mom said as she passed him on the way into the house.

"My other brother," he answered, giving her the same excuse he had used since he was five years old.

*****

Later, after the take-out had been consumed and the paper plates shoved into the garbage, Colton brought two beers to the living room; setting one beside his mother who was pushed back in her re-cliner reading a new celebrity magazine. He carried his to the couch and took a long pull before sitting it on the coffee table beside his stockinged feet balanced on its edge.

Cinnamon crawled up and settled on his stomach. Staring into space, he automatically stroked her while a small smile played around his mouth.

Finally, his mother lowered her magazine and looked at him over her glasses. "So who is she?"

Startled, he looked back at her. "What are you talking about?"

"You're sitting there grinning like an idiot at absolutely nothing so I am assuming somebody jingled your bell. I'm just wondering who it is."

He was unable to keep a smile from reappearing as he looked down at the cat. "An artist."

"I thought you had sworn off of women for the time being and where would you meet an artist?" There was a trace of disquiet in his mother's voice.

"Her gallery was right across from one of the houses I was checking out as a possible renovation project. I went over to see if somebody there knew anything about it."

"And so what do you know about this 'artist'?"

"Her eyes are the same blue as Cin's," he said softly.

His mother studied his face. His expression had a dreamy distant quality to it; like something more than lust was drifting in his blood.

She looked away. That was ridiculous. You don't fall for someone just meeting them once. Then she was chided by her memory. "You did." Yes, she had. And it was the biggest mistake of her life; one she would do anything to prevent him from repeating.

*****

After Mya roamed the kitchen trying to figure out what to fix for dinner, she settled for making a piece of toast. Her stomach had a funny feel to it. She probed the sensation, wondering if some bug had caught up with her. Careful consideration told her it was butterflies, not bugs. The sensation puzzled her. There was nothing in the immediate future to warrant the feeling.

She washed her dish and made a cup of chamomile/lavender tea; carrying it as she doubled-checked the doors were locked before climbing to her workroom. At the top of the stairs, she flipped the switch turning off the downstairs lights.

She pulled her journal out from under the rotating pile of sketchbooks stacked on a shelf. She hadn't written in it for a while, but it was always her go-to choice when whatever was banging around in her brain needed examination. Setting it beside her tea, she reached for a pen.

Putting the nib against the paper, she found herself sketching instead of writing. When she lifted the pen, a face looked back at her from the paper. Thick hair, angular jaw, dark eyes, and a mouth she had had a hard time keeping her eyes off of earlier now stared up at her. She lightly stroked in the beginnings of a beard.

Now her butterflies made sense. This guy had somehow managed to slip past her barriers—okay, maybe just the first barrier, but still it was enough to surprise her.

She knew from painful past experience a relationship was not good for her art and she was not good in a relationship because of her art. There just didn't seem to be enough of her to go around. Eventually she was shorting her work to give more attention to someone, and, when she didn't, things soured and decayed into a pathetic pile of pain.

There was no reason to even open herself to the possibility of one. At twenty-five years of age, she had finally managed to make a life that worked. All the people on her carefully curated list of friends 'got her' because they were themselves engaged in soul-defining activities.

She loved Tin Roof Gallery. There was not one square inch of it that didn't have her handprints all over it. Every single decision regarding its renovation had been in support of her art.

She looked back down at the drawing, lightly tracing the outline of the face with her finger. Finally, she picked up her pen again and began to write.

To the stunningly sexy man who wandered through my front door today. Although it may seem presumptuous to believe you would have any further interest beyond the hour we spent tonight, it is best we have no further contact. While you are very easy on the eyes and exhibit charming old-school manners, I must confess I am already committed.

Its arms were the ones sheltering me during the very long and lonely days of my growing up. When everything else failed me, it was always there. After all these years, we share a single heartbeat and it is the fabric of my soul. I am necessary to it, and without my hands, my eyes, it cannot bring itself into being.

Tonight has warned me you are very dangerous. Stupid as it sounds, I might actually think about making room in my life for you if you were to come around again. And that is why I must never let you back through my door, Colton Williams.

Pushing her pen back in the jar, she studied the face a minute longer. Then putting her finger to her own lips, she touched it to the mouth of the drawing before closing the journal.

*****

She was seated cross-legged on the floor the next afternoon surrounded by open plastic totes and piles of fabric scraps she was sorting when the door opened and Colton leaned in.

"Hi, did I by any chance leave my clipboard here last night?" he asked.

She smiled warmly; totally annoyed with herself at how excited she was inside to see him again. "You did." She pointed to it lying neatly at the end of the counter.

He came fully inside and closed the door.

"You know, you're wearing two different socks."

She stretched her legs out, examining the pink and yellow striped sock on her right foot and the orange sock with lime green polka-dots on her left-foot.

"I loathe matching up socks so I just toss them in a basket. The first two I pull out are what I wear. Nobody sees them but me, so it's okay."

"What are you doing?" he asked gesturing to the fabric.

"I was just eyeballing my inventory before the flea market this weekend. I usually try to pick up fabric there and I get really perturbed with myself when I bring home colors I already have a lot of."

She sat aside the items in her lap, shifting to stand up.

He shoved up the sleeves on his faded waffle weave Henley, and reached out a hand to her. As she took his proffered hand, she noticed his arm. "What happened?" she asked, looking at the gash angling across his forearm.

Pulling her easily to her feet, he shrugged. "There was a knot in a two by four. The board bucked when I hit it with the power saw."

"Did you put anything on it?"

"I poured some water over it."

Taking it in her hands, she lifted his arm to examine it closer. "I have some stuff that is great for wounds. Come on."

He followed her into the kitchen. Like every other area of the downstairs he had seen, it was immaculate. She motioned him to the sink while she went to a very large storage hutch standing against the back wall.

Opening a bottom door, she pulled out a white plastic bin with a large red cross emblazoned on the side. She carried it to the counter by the sink. Rummaging around, she pulled out a bottle of hydrogen peroxide, cotton balls, and a blue jar.

He watched her hands as she doctored his arm. Slender with long fingers; the nails were short but neatly manicured. Her touch was light as she first cleaned the wound and then slathered a layer of salve over it. When she pulled out a packaged gauze square, he pulled his arm away and started to pull down his sleeve.

"I think I'm good now."

She pushed his hand away. "Sorry, you're not done yet. If you don't put the gauze over it, you're going to get salve all over your shirt which isn't where you need it."

She secured the gauze with a couple of strips of paper tape. "These don't pull so badly when you take them off."

Noting the well-stocked bin, "You must patch up a lot of people with all the stuff you have," he said.

She laughed as she put everything back and picked it up. "Most of it is left over from when we were working on this place. Although they were sincere and worked really hard, construction is just not what my friends do; consequently there were lots of boo-boos along the way. Fortunately, we got it done before anyone lost a body part. Although if you ever meet Aaron, he will be glad to regale you with the story of a killer sliver he swears almost cost him his finger."

Colton found himself paying serious attention to her bottom when she bent over to put the bin away. He flushed when she stood and turned, almost catching him.

He followed as she padded back to the main room. Seeing the fabric again prompted him to ask, "So where is the flea market?"

Perching on the counter, she drew her legs up. "It's in the parking lot outside the old Bingham auto sales building on the other end of town."

"That's a little bit of a trek," he commented.

"It's not bad. The bus stops just a block away. And sometimes I can get a friend to bring me back."

"You don't drive?"

"Yes, of course, I do. I just don't have a car right now. In the renovation, I ran into a few things I hadn't budgeted for so I sold my car to get it finished."

"How do you get around?"

She shrugged. "I walk, take the bus, and occasionally cadge a ride from somebody. It all works out."

"So what time would you like me to pick you up?"

"Oh, I wasn't angling for a ride, really."

He smiled. "I was going to ask you if you were available to do something this weekend, so if you don't mind the company, I would like to take you to the flea market."

The impish sparkle was back in her eyes. "I will issue a warning right now. The market is filled with friends who are, er, a little out there. Actually, some of them are really flat out weird. Are you okay with that?"

"Ever see what shows up on construction crews? I think I'll be good."

"It opens at ten. I like to be there when it opens otherwise all the good stuff gets picked over fast. So is nine thirty too early?"

His answering smile burned right into her chest, leaving a warm glow. He headed to the door. "Nine thirty Saturday. I'll be here."

Her hand bumped the clipboard as she turned to watch him leave out the window. Grabbing it, she threw open the door.

"Colton!" she said, waving it when he turned back.

He bounded up the stairs.

She tucked the board under his arm. "By the way, dress warm. It's open air."

He wanted to reach out and touch her face so badly, he jammed his thumbs in his pockets to keep his hands under control.

She turned back to the door, her long braid swinging behind her while he edged his way back to the stairs.

As soon as she was back inside, she peeked out the door window to watch him getting in his pickup. Turning away, she leaned against the door and gave herself a warning. "Girl, you are playing with dynamite and I will have no sympathy if you get your damn hands blown off."

As he headed home, Colton was totally aware something inside of him was pumping its fist in the air and shouting, "Yeah!"

Chapter 3

She must have been watching for him because as soon as he pulled his pickup to the curb, Mya stepped out of the gallery and began locking the door. He slid out and met her half-way up the walk.

A blue sweater extended a good eight inches below the edge of her bomber jacket, covering much of her bottom while the turtle neck extended almost to her jawline, a scarf wrapped over it. He was happy to see her braided hair hanging over her shoulder. She was carrying a Hello Miss Kitty backpack. Taking it from her, he held it up while raising an eyebrow.

"It represents cheapness, as in only $3.00 on the clearance table, not artistic taste. And how's the arm?" she asked as she touched the sleeve of his jean jacket. "It's good. You were right, the stuff you put on it practically healed it by the next morning."

He held the door open as she climbed in the pickup. Although he had dragged most of the debris out of it, it was still covered in a fine haze of construction dirt and sawdust, which didn't seem to faze her.

Climbing in on the other side, he tucked the backpack between them. There was something careful and reticent about her. It made him want to move slowly so as not to startle her into disappearing.

"Oh, oh," he said on the drive over. "It looks like ice in the rain. It's apt to be pretty chilly at the market."

Mya leaned forward to look through windshield. "Darn. That will totally hurt business today." She turned a small smile on him. "The flea market is a big part of some of my friends' income. No people. No money."

21

He gave her a reassuring smile. "It is spring in Oregon so it could be 80 degrees by this afternoon."

She nodded. "It's like Mother Nature stands in front of her closet this time of year trying on different outfits, and can't make up her mind."

He gave her a quick glance. Her way of looking at the world was different from anyone he had ever met. "At least, you shouldn't have to fight anyone to get a good parking spot. Summer, parking pretty much resembles *Death Race 2000*."

He slipped the truck into a spot right next to the flea market. "You're right," he said as he cut the ignition.

She had already hopped out of the truck, dragging her backpack after her by the time he was able to exit the truck and come around. She flipped her braid over her shoulder before slipping the backpack over it. "Ready?"

Leading the way, she headed into the maze of canopies. They had only made it a little way in when she was stopped short, her head snapping back. She whirled as did Colton, his fist unconsciously clenching. A huge black man stood holding the end of Mya's braid. "Duncan!" She flung herself in the man's arms. His hug lifted her about two feet off the pavement.

"How many times do I have to tell you that name is not to be used on the weekends? You're gonna ruin my image."

"Yeah, whatever. How's Anita?"

"All big belly and swollen feet, and would you believe she sent me out at one a.m. in the morning to try to find her some licorice ice cream. Girl, she does not even like licorice!"

"So do we have colors yet?"

He reached into his coat pocket, pulling out his smartphone. Flicking his thumb through the icons, he eventually handed it to Mya. She studied it. "So its peony pink and butter yellow. Do we have a theme?"

"Carousel. We're gonna go with carousel because she found one at Babies R Us and just had to have it. Don't know why babies have to have themes. I was ninth out of ten kids and shared my room with four brothers and we didn't have themes."

"You were third out of three, and, since you were the only boy, you had a room to yourself done up in Transformers. Shonda and

Monique shared a bedroom which was all Lisa Frank."

"My story's better." Noticing Colton standing close to her watching, he held out his hand. "Sorry. I didn't mean to be rude. I'm..."

Taking his hand, Colton finished "Cool Train. You've been the DJ at some events I've been to. You do an awesome job, man."

"Thanks, it's nice to meet someone who appreciates talent," Duncan said, tossing a look to Mya who answered by rolling her eyes. "And speaking of which, I'm pulling a new gig starting next Saturday at the Caverns." He patted his pockets, finally pulling a card and a pen out. He motioned for Mya to turn around. Using her shoulder, he scribbled something on it, then handed it to Colton. "That will get two in for free, even if one of them is her."

Handing him back his phone, Mya stood on tiptoe to kiss him on the cheek. "Catch you later, Duncan," she said slightly emphasizing his name. "Give my love to Anita."

As they turned and began moving deeper into the market, Colton asked. "So how long have known him?"

"Since the first grade. We were in school together. Anita was my locker partner clear through high school. Duncan's the one who wired the gallery. He's a licensed electrician during the day. DJing is his passion, but it doesn't pay a family man's bills. First stop," she said as she pointed to a booth.

As they approached, an elderly man in a wheelchair was unloading trays full of silver objects out of a case onto the table in front of him. "Hola, Señor Munoz."

"Hola, Mya. Cómo está usted?"

"Muy bien. And we have now reached the end of my Spanish. Where's your helper today? "

"The twins, they have soccer practice. Diego will come when it is over."

He lifted another tray and shakily placed it on the table. Mya reached out to grab his hands. "You're freezing," she said.

"Sí, muy frío. The man with the weather did not say muy frío. "

Mya dug in her pocket and brought a five dollar bill. "Colton, there is coffee booth about five stalls up. Would you get a large cup for Señor Munoz?" Shoving the money in his hands, she circled around the booth, unwrapping her scarf.

After hesitating for a moment, Colton ventured off. When he returned with the steaming cup in its sleeve, he found Señor Munoz with Mya's scarf wrapped around his neck. Her fingerless gloves were on his hands. She had found a blanket somewhere and had it tucked around his knees.

Colton reached across the table and handed the elderly man the cup. He opened his hand, setting several packets of sugar and creamer on the table.

"Dos azúcar, por favor."

Mya popped the lid on the coffee and poured two packages of sugar in. Putting the lid back on, she covered the sipping hole with her thumb and gave the coffee a couple of good swirls before handing it to the older gentleman.

He sipped gratefully. "Gracias, gracias, Mya y amigo."

She gave him a quick hug of his shoulders. "Tell Diego hola," she said before circling back to the walkway.

"What is it he sells?" Colton asked.

"Milagros, miracle medals. I use them sometimes in my work. Diego, his grandson, is good about tucking back some of the unusual ones for me."

As they passed various booths without even slowing, he observed, "It appears you have a plan."

She grinned. "Actually I do. I hit the booths where I get all my best stuff first, then wander around just to see who and what is new. And our first stop is just ahead."

Colton looked side to side as they traipsed along until Mya tugged at his jacket sleeve, nodding her head toward a stall filled with vintage records.

"Hey, lovely lady," called the distinguished-looking man standing behind tables loaded with vinyl record-filled wooden crates.

"Hi, Aaron. Anything new I should own?"

He shook his head. "Nothing has come in yet, but I think I have a line on a Super Session album. Still working on it."

"Awesome. I guess if there's nothing new, I'll catch you next time." Turning to go she was stopped by another man calling. "Mya! Mya! Wait."

A short, chunky middle-aged man carrying two coffee containers was hurrying in their direction. Skidding to stop in front of her, he turned and thrust both cups at Colton who took them with a startled expression.

"Mya, look." The man held out his left hand flashing a silver band on his ring finger. "He asked me, girl! I'm engaged. Aaron and I going to get married. Say you'll be my maid of honor, please, please, please!" he asked bouncing on his toes.

She gave him a hug, and reached over the boxes to hug the other man. "Congratulations, you two. And I will definitely be your maid of honor, Eric. When's the wedding?"

The short man stopped bouncing. "Well, we're still in negotiations about the date. I want Christmas when everything is all sparkly and champagney. Aaron wants Valentine's Day because it's so uber-romantic. What do you think?"

"Halloween and a Nightmare before Christmas theme?"

"You are so useless in helping settle arguments," the man sniffed as he turned to retrieve the coffees. Reaching for them, he actually noticed Colton. "Oh, god, you are totally gorgeous!" he said as he looked him up and down.

Colton shot a panicked look to Mya just as Aaron reached over the records and popped the man on the back of the head. "We can settle the argument by cancelling the wedding, too, bitch," he said grabbing for one of the containers.

Mya was grinning as she reached out and hooked Colton's hand with her fingertips, tugging him after her. "Kelly's next." He tried to catch hold of her hand, but she pulled away before he was able to get a grip.

"And Kelly sells?"

"Vintage fabric, patterns, and notions. She has the most incredible stuff."

They cut between two booths, crossing to the next row of vendors. A little way along they came to a booth with tables on three sides. A tall, broad-shouldered person Colton guessed might be a woman stood in the center. Her hair was buzz cut and dyed an improbable orange. Tats were visible in the opening of the denim shirt she wore and under her pushed up sleeves. When she straightened up, Colton realized the woman easily matched his six foot height.

"What's new and amazing this month, Kelly?"

"How about Peter Max?"

Mya's mouth fell open. "Are you kidding me?"

"Nope." The woman bent over, rummaging under the table, bringing out a several pieces. Mya unfolded them and looked them over. "Oh, yeah, I want these. And I need some green and pink. And will you please remind me why I have about fifty shades of yellow?"

"Cuz I'm a helleva a saleswoman."

"No kidding. The only thing I give more money to is my mortgage payment."

Colton watched the two women as they poked among the stacks of fabric. Mya's face was a study in thoughtfulness as she flipped colors over each other; inexplicably squeezed the fabric; and held it up in light.

She had just handed her choices over for Kelly to tally and bag when a rumpus of children's voices engulfed them. Colton looked past Mya to see aman carrying a toddler following in the wake of three children bee lining in their direction. The three swarmed around Mya, jumping up and down to get her attention. When the man arrived, Mya reached for the one in his arms. Handing him off, he circled around and leaned over the table to lay a passionate kiss on the woman behind it.

Colton was amused to see he was nearly a head shorter.

"Did you tell Mya the news yet?" the man said.

"Oh, yeah. There's another bun baking and the total is $76.00."

Mya started. "Geez, guys, what are you going for? World domination?"

The man rubbed his chin. "Now there's an idea."

"Uh-huh. The factory is being closed after this one."

Colton spoke. "Excuse me, but I think you have a runaway." He pointed at a small child who was hotfooting it away.

"Get her, Steve, before she falls in the pho kettle."

The man took off at a trot.

Mya tried to reach for her backpack, but was unable to manage with the toddler in her arms. Looking around a moment, she handed him to Colton with a sweet smile, before pulling her backpack off her shoulder and turning her attention to Kelly.

Colton felt a tug on his jean jacket. Turning slightly, he saw a little girl earnestly looking up at him. "Hi. That's Mya" she said pointing. "Mya is our friend. Is she your friend, too?"

"Yes, I hope she is," Colton answered as he gently bounced the little boy in his arms.

"What's your name?"

"Colton."

"It's almost like mine!" she answered excitedly. "My name is Colleen."

Just then the man returned with the child tucked firmly under his arm. He handed the child off to his wife and reached for the toddler.

He held out his hand to Colton. "Hi, I'm Steve, and this is my wife, Kelly."

Colton responded as soon as his hand was empty. The little girl, who had remained by his side, said, "His name is Colton so it's almost like mine."

"Yes, it is," her father answered.

"Okay, guys, I'm done. Who has a goodbye hug for me?" Mya asked as she finished zipping the bag of material inside her backpack.

After hugging Mya, the little girl insisted on giving Colton a hug as well.

"I think you found a new friend in Colleen," Mya said as they walked away. "Thank you for being so tolerant with the chaos that is the Barrett family. Hanging with them is somewhere between a three-ring circus and a full-on war zone."

"They're kinda an odd-couple."

Mya nodded. "That's an understatement. Kelly served as a mechanic in the transportation division of the Marines. Steve was this little nerd working IT when they met because of a fender bender. He drifted through a stop sign and banged into her car. Steve told me when he got out of the car, he thought a goddess was emerging from the vehicle he hit. Kelly said her first thought when he got out was she could take him without breaking a sweat."

Colton laughed.

"What's next?" he asked.

Mya stopped, tugging up the hem of her sweater to fish in her jean pocket. Colton reached in his jacket pocket. Looking up, after she had extracted a slip of paper, she saw him holding the five dollar bill she had given him between two fingers. He carefully tucked it back into her pocket. She was startled at how aware she was of his touch near her hip.

She covered by holding up the list. "That Sixties' Place."

Once again they cut between booths and headed to the end of the last row. The booth they headed towards could truly have time-travelled in from the prior century. It had all the funkiness of the actual sixties.

A short, stocky woman dressed in a tie-dyed sweat- shirt over a denim shirt was busy arranging various items on the table. When she turned, Colton noted her long grey-white braid was slightly longer than Mya's, reaching past her hips.

Two teenagers in the booth were moving boxes and helping set out items when they approached.

"Mya!" the girl squealed when she saw them. The older woman's head whipped in their direction before she squeezed out between the tables, holding her arms wide. The two women embraced with obvious great affection.

Colton stopped a respectful distance from them. Looking over Mya's shoulder, the woman smiled at him. She had a face that looked like it lived a contented life. When they released their hold on each other, the woman gestured toward Colton. Mya waved him over. "Emma, this is Colton. Colton, Emma."

Emma gripped his hand in both of hers. "Delighted to meet you," she said. "Mya is like another of my grandchildren."

"Where's Seth?" Mya asked.

"We finally hogtied him long enough to get his hip replaced. He is still under restrictions so he's being watched by Barb and Jeremy; both of whom are big enough to sit on him, if necessary. So what are you weaving?"

Mya moved to the table as Emma slipped back behind it. "Unfortunately, nothing at the moment, other than my spider thing which is so not cooperating. I had a couple of quilt commissions which are now finished. You?"

"I have the loom warped but with Seth's surgery and starting all the spring work around the farm, I haven't even filled my shuttles. I have rugs I'm hooking when I have a minute."

While they were talking, Mya was searching through a number of brown bottles set on a beautifully stained and polished wooden display. She placed four of them on the table.

Emma picked them up. "Geranium, clary sage, bergamot, and neroli. These are all working oils. Remember you need to balance with relaxation, too." She reached over and added another bottle. "Lavender."

"What are those, Stacy?" Mya asked pointing to packages filled with powdery looking balls.

"Bath bombs. I made them myself," the girl said proudly.

"What fragrances?"

"Jasmine, rose, and ylang-ylang."

Stacy leaned over the table to whisper in Mya's ear. "The guy you're with is a total stud muffin, you might want to try the ylang-ylang. Grandma says it's an aphrodisiac."

Mya laughed and hugged the girl. "Excellent suggestion. In fact, give me three of each."

Stacy began to carefully place the balls into plastic bags along with a little card identifying their fragrance. When she had loaded the bags and placed them next to the bottles, she leaned back over the table again. "Let me know how it works. There's this guy in English 121 and I might have to try it myself."

Mya whispered something back in answer.

"Done."

As Mya circled back to the front of the booth, Stacy started to load the items she had selected into a bag and tot up their prices on a calculator.

"So have you eaten today?" Emma asked Mya.

Colton was surprised when Mya and the two teens started laughing.

Stacy explained it. "Grandma has this thing about feeding everything that moves. If a chicken walks by the back door at her house, she'll ask it if it has eaten."

"In my defense," Emma said, "Mya is notorious for getting so involved in her work she forgets to eat. I have had to have Seth physically drag her out of the studio to get some victuals down her gullet on many occasions. Am I right?"

Looking a bit sheepish, Mya nodded. "But I'm getting better." Emma gave her a hard look. "Sorta," she confessed.

Several people were now converging on the booth. Mya handed over her debit card. Stacy ran it through the Square on her grandmother's cell phone and then held the phone out for Mya to sign.

Gathering up the bag, Mya moved away to make room for new arrivals. Emma called after them. "Nice to meet you, Colton. See she eats."

Mya looked at him. "My eating habits are not your concern."

"Maybe not, but right now food sounds good to me. How about you?"

He watched as she actually seemed to have to think about it. "I'm starved," she said.

"You want to get something here or go somewhere?"

She rubbed her hands together. "Inside and warm would be awesome."

He wrapped his hands around her cold fingers; blowing his warm breath over them. "Cactus Flats okay? They have an amazing…"

"Nacho," they said simultaneously and grinned at one another.

Turning in the direction of the street, they encountered an influx of other flea market attendees. Colton noted the number of men who were giving Mya the eye. He glanced at her. She wasn't paying any attention, until one man deliberately maneuvered to bump into her. The guy used the moment to try to start a conversation while apologizing. Colton moved in and cupped his hand around the back of Mya's neck pulling her closer to him. The two men exchanged looks of territoriality. Colton slightly lifted his chin in challenge. The other man backed down with a mumbled "sorry," and moved back into the crowd. Colton kept his hand firmly in place until they reached his truck and he had safely secured her inside.

At the diner, they placed their order. When Mya's cup of Earl Grey tea arrived, he watched as she wrapped her hands around it, and, closing her eyes, breathed in the steamy aroma. Finally, she sipped it. Somehow it felt incredibly sensuous.

Catching the intensity of his gaze when she looked up at him, a lovely bloom of color rose in her cheeks. Suddenly, she turned her head slightly and stared into space for a long moment. He had the weird sensation part of her was no longer sitting in the booth across from him.

Unzipping her jacket, she reached into an inner pocket and pulled out a small sketch book and a mechanical pencil. Clicking it a couple of times, she bent her head as her hand began to flash over the paper.

He watched elements of a drawing appear. She sat back and stared at it for a moment, then leaned forward adding a couple of pencil strokes. She tucked the pencil back in her pocket and picked up the book.

He held out his hand. "May I?"

Mya handed it over just as the nacho arrived.

The small drawing clearly showed a carousel in the center of the page empty of its usual creatures. Instead, they were asleep among the leaves and foliage watched over by the moon and stars. It was beautifully rendered for something she appeared to have hastily sketched. He handed the sketchbook back.

She shoved a loaded tortilla chip in her mouth; wiping her fingers before taking the book and stuffing it back in her pocket.

"Anita's baby shower is next Sunday and since it took forever for her to choose a theme, I only have a week to get a quilted wall hanging done. But, at least, I have a place to start now."

"Do you do that often?" he asked. She looked at him puzzled.

"You just kind a disappeared there for a minute. Just before you started drawing."

She thoughtfully bit into another chip. "I don't know. Being alone most of the time, I don't really know what I do."

"You don't date?"

"I haven't for a long time. After I bought the house, there was no time and definitely no energy. I was working about sixteen to eighteen hours a day between the renovation and keeping up with commission work to pay for it all. I was lucky some days if I managed to get showered before falling into bed. Guys aren't exactly attracted to zombies, especially dirty, smelly ones, and that was pretty much what I was for the better part of two years."

He nodded. "I get that. When the weather improves, we're on the job from first light until late most days. It totally messes with a social life. I end up just hanging out and sleeping with Cin."

He caught her dimming smile and grinned. "Cinnamon is my Siamese cat."

"So you are in a relationship."

"I like to think so, but I'm not sure how committed she is. Truth is I'm pretty sure if somebody showed up with a case of tuna, Cin would drop me in a heartbeat." The conversation maintained its light, impersonal tone through the remaining nacho and the ride back to Mya's gallery.

Pulling up in front, Colton grabbed her backpack which was once again between them; sliding it onto his own shoulder. Coming around the truck, she was already out and waiting on the sidewalk. She reached for Miss Kitty, but he shook his head. "To the door, remember?"

He kept the backpack over his shoulder and wished he could think of a reason to touch her again. At the door, he slipped it off, and slid it on her shoulder. "Key?"

She pulled it out of her pocket so he could unlock the door. After handing her key back, he ran his knuckle lightly along her jaw line, ending with a tender tap to her chin.

"You take care," he said and headed back to the truck before she could thank him.

She slipped inside and closed the door; standing still until she heard the truck engine start and pull away before heading upstairs. Dumping Miss Kitty on her work table, she shrugged out of her jacket, hanging it on the coat tree. After pulling her purchases out, she held Miss Kitty up and spoke to her.

"I am definitely the speed dating champ, girl." She glanced at her cell phone, noting the time. "You're going to have to admit five and half hours of togetherness from the first time I saw him to to-day's goodbye may be a new record." She stared at the backpack for a moment. "Yeah, it's not funny to me either."

Chapter 4

Reflecting on the drive home, Colton realized he didn't know one thing more about Mya than he had after their first beer, other than the people she had introduced him to at the market. Usually at this point, women had provided him with plenty of information to use if he decided he was interested enough to continue seeing them. His usual game plan, honed through years of chasing, catching, kissing, and bedding women, was not giving him the results he was used to. She hadn't asked when she would see him again or even offered her phone number; the usual reactions to his noncommittal farewell. There was nothing to give him a clue about whether there was any reciprocating interest in him or not. She was turning out to be a beautiful, quirky mystery.

Colton pulled the truck in against the curb in front of the house since his mother's car was in the single driveway. He glanced over at the passenger seat as he opened his door. Sitting neatly in the middle of it was a small blue jar. He was pretty sure he knew what it was before he picked it up. He smiled after reading the label identifying it as 'wound salve'. He found the quiet, unexpected gesture incredibly endearing. He tucked the jar inside the glove compartment before heading into the house. Its meaning was between Mya and himself, and something made him want to keep it that way.

His mom glanced up from the Sudoku puzzle she was working. "As long as you are up, get me a beer."

He came back from the kitchen with two; setting one beside her before taking his to the couch. He pulled his cell phone out of his jean jacket pocket and dropped it on the coffee table.

"So where'd you go so early this morning?"

33

"The flea market."

His mother looked at him. "Flea market? What possessed you to go to the flea market?"

"I gave someone a ride."

His mother stared at him for a long moment, her eyebrows drawn together. "The artist." She laid her puzzle in her lap. "You saw the artist again."

"I'm a big boy now, Mom. I can see whoever I want," he answered mildly.

She looked back down at her puzzle. "Well, I just hope she isn't one of those who calls or texts you a thousand times a day like…"

"Tiffany?"

"Tiffany was just insecure about your relationship."

"Insecure about our relationship or afraid I would find out she was banging the potato chip salesman at the same time?"

"I hear things didn't work out so well. And FYI, she is coming back to work at Deuce's starting Monday. You know, in case you want to stop by or something."

Colton reached for his beer. He had never understood his mother's obsession in trying to hook him with every unmarried female who came to work with her at the convenience store.

He changed subjects. "I did meet Cool Train at the market. You know, the DJ who was at our company picnic last year. He's got a new gig going and he gave me a pass to his show."

"Want me to see if Tiffany would be free to go?"

Colton stood up. "Mom, let's get this straight. Tiffany is ancient history, in like I have no intention of ever going there again. Got it?"

He picked up his bottle and headed to his bedroom. In a few minutes, she heard his TV go on and the sound of one of his video games begin before it went quiet indicating he had plugged in his earphones.

Putting the leg rest to her recliner down, she crossed to the coffee table and picked up his phone. She quickly thumbed through his contacts, recent messages, and even the few photos he had. There was nothing she didn't already know. She carefully put the phone back with a puzzled expression. If he was so smitten with this person, why was there no evidence she actually existed?

Chapter 5

The beginning of the week found Mother Nature teasing summer with the weather turning warm and dry. The construction crew took full advantage of it, not quitting until after six at night. Colton made several trips by the gallery, but the open sign was always off and the lights dimmed in the bottom floor.

On Thursday, the inspector, who had to sign off so they could proceed with the next phase, hadn't shown so the crew was sent home at four p.m. Colton made a dash to his house to shower and change clothes before heading in the direction of the gallery.

When he pulled up in front, he was relieved to see the open sign on and the first floor lit up. Hopping out of the truck, he jogged toward the door, taking the stairs two at a time. Glancing through the window by the counter, he saw Mya sitting cross-legged on the floor; head down as she stitched on the large piece of material draped over her lap.

He watched her expression anxiously as he pushed through the front door. "Hi," he said tentatively.

"Colton!" The warmth in her smile was tangible.

She thrust the work in her lap aside and jumped up as he came around to where she was sitting. Suddenly, with a small, inarticulate sound, she started to fall, reaching ineffectively for the counter.

Colton grabbed her upper arms and pulled her into him. "Mya?"

She laid her forehead against his shoulder, resting her hands flat on his chest. With the barest turn of his head, he could smell the sweet cleanness of her hair; feel it under his chin.

Drawing a deep breath, she pushed away and raised her head. "I am so sorry," she apologized. "I was sitting too long and got up too

35

fast. Made myself light-headed for a moment." She looked genuinely embarrassed.

Even though she was pulling back from him, he was reluctant to let go. In fact, all he wanted to do was pull her back tight against him and hold her there for like, maybe, a decade or two. Instead, he let his hands slide off her arms, crossing them over his chest.

"So have you eaten today?" he asked.

She threw her head back and laughed. "Yes, I have, Emma."

"When and what?"

"You sound just like her. I had half a bagel with blueberry spread for breakfast at 6 a.m., thank you very much."

He pulled his cell phone out of his pocket; holding it up for her to see. "You know it is now five sixteen. It is possible you really should eat again before the day is over."

She glanced at the pile of fabric on the floor. "I'll get something later. I still have a ton of stitching to do on the shower gift."

"How about you stitch and I rustle up something?" Colton headed to the kitchen. "I can cook."

"Hmmm, that isn't going to work very well," she said, biting her lip. "There's not much to rustle. I haven't taken time to go to the store this week."

In the kitchen, he opened the refrigerator which was sparkling clean in its emptiness. The cupboards held little other than various teas.

"You need a keeper. You obviously suck at being left on your own. I'll be back," he said as he headed to the door. He paused and looked back at her, "Don't lock me out, please."

Watching out the window, she saw him trot down the stairs. In a moment, his truck started and pulled away from the curb. She turned on the task light attached to the counter, sat down on the floor, and picked up the quilt. But instead of stitching, she looked at her hands, feeling again the warm, broadness of his chest under them. "I think I'd rather find a way to lock you in," she thought wistfully as she picked up her needle and began pushing it through the fabric.

She lost track of time as she appliqued a giraffe head onto the quilt. She inadvertently started and stuck her finger with the needle when someone attempted to open her front door; apparently without success.

She got up and looked through the window before pulling it open. Colton was standing there with a pizza box in one hand, a grocery bag in his arm, and a six pack of beer in his other hand. He stepped in and set the pizza on the counter, then shifting the grocery bag, he headed to the kitchen. Mya followed.

He put the bag on the counter and began to unload it. There was a quart of milk, a dozen eggs, plain and raisin bagels, peanut butter, Marion berry fruit spread plus two apples and two oranges.

Mya watched wide-eyed. "Oh, my. You totally did not have to do that. But thank you so much and how much do I owe you?"

"Your company on Saturday to see Cool Train at the Caverns," Colton said. He reached out and lightly took her hand, pulling her toward the main room. "Let's eat. I'm starved. Hope the Gatling from Capone's works for you."

She stopped still. "It's my favorite. How did you know?"

"Your refrigerator."

She looked confused as she glanced back into her kitchen.

"The menu on the door. You had it underlined," he said as he pulled napkins out of his pocket, and handed her a couple before flipping the lid open on the box.

There was still a quarter of a pizza in the box when they were both satiated. Colton picked it up and carried it to the refrigerator. He returned from the kitchen with a beer. Mya had again picked up her project. Looking at her feet, he was amused to see she had a light blue sock covered with pink pigs on one and a white sock with candy canes on the other.

He sat down and watched as her needle flashed in and out of the material.

"Did you go to art school to learn all this?"

She shook her head without looking up. "I would have loved to go to art school but didn't have the means. Between Nancy's grandmother and Emma, though, I think I still managed to get some awesome training."

"Nancy's the counselor, right?"

"Yes. I grew up across the street from her family and spent a huge amount of time there. Her grandmother was a master quilter. She helped me make my first quilts, showing me proper techniques and tricks. She also taught me just how much material you could find in thrift shops, garage sales, and flea markets. She helped me build my first stash that way. It just kills me now if I have to pay retail price for something at the fabric store. Material is expensive."

"And Emma is a weaver?"

Mya flashed an impressed expression at him. "You really do pay attention, don't you?"

He smiled. "How did you meet her?"

"When I was fourteen, I got hired to help with art projects for the little kids in the summer community program."

"I thought you had to be sixteen to get hired in the program. At least, it's what the stuff they distributed at high school said."

She blushed. "There may or may not have been some falsification in the application process."

"You lied about your age?"

"I needed a job and couldn't wait until I was sixteen so I fibbed on my birthdate. Anyway, as part of the program, Emma was teaching simple weaving projects. I was assigned as her helper and totally fell in love with it. I started trying to do my own stuff and kept coming to her with questions. She finally decided I should come out to her studio on the farm. Beginning in the fall, Seth would pick me up every Friday night and bring me back Sunday morning. I helped around the farm, and Emma would teach me using the looms in her studio. We did that until I was able to legally get a job at a burger place."

"And the painting?"

She shrugged. "High school art classes and YouTube videos on techniques, mostly."

She snipped the thread and stuck the needle in a pincushion, before closing her eyes and rolling her shoulders. "Memo to me: binge stitching makes the body cranky."

"Turn around," Colton said.

When she looked at him blankly, he moved his finger in a circle. She complied. He swung his legs so they were positioned on either side of her. Placing his hands on her waist he pulled her back into the V his legs formed. Moving his hands up, he began to massage her shoulders and neck. After a few moments, she relaxed the way Cin did when he stroked her.

His body suddenly took notice of how close her bottom was to his crotch and heat began to rise in him.

"Better?" he asked, sliding back as his jeans became uncomfortably tight.

"Awesome," she said, rotating her neck. "Thank you."

He picked up his empty beer bottle and headed to the kitchen.

"So what time should I pick you up?" he asked, leaning against the kitchen door jamb upon his return. "I'm thinking the music starts at eight and since Cool is pretty popular, it's going to be packed. Might be hard to get a table unless we get there when the doors open."

She grinned at him and reached under the counter for her cell phone. Opening an app, she speedily typed something in before setting it beside her leg. Within a few minutes, the phone buzzed and she picked it up.

"Duncan said he will reserve us a table in the best location, but he wants to know if maybe you couldn't do better than me for a date?"

"Well, I do still have two days. I'll see who shows up at the construction site tomorrow. Speaking of which, tomorrow is gonna be a long day if the inspector comes and signs off."

He headed for the door while Mya scrambled to her feet to follow.

Opening it, he turned back. "See you Saturday at seven." He leaned in and lightly kissed her forehead. "Goodnight, Mya. Lock the door."

She watched through the ajar door until she heard his truck door slam before she closed it and turned the lock. Leaning against it, she touched the place his lips had touched.

Chapter 6

Colton spent Saturday detailing the interior of his truck. Somehow the planned evening felt like a real old-school date, and even if she wore jeans, he wanted Mya to see he had thought of her.

His mother watched bemused as he scrubbed and polished his truck to a state of cleanliness it hadn't been in since the day he drove it home. She was further surprised at the amount of time he spent getting ready. When he finally emerged from his room at six-thirty, she realized her son had matured into an extremely handsome man.

"Bye," he said, not even looking at her. "See you later."

She pursed her lips in a small smile. "Maybe not as 'later' as you think." It was high time she got a look at the outsider who apparently had captured her son's fancy. She picked up her phone, scrolled through her contact list, and pressed Babs' number.

*****

The downstairs of the gallery blazed with light. Colton opened the door. "Mya?"

"Just a moment," she called from upstairs.

He leaned against the counter, prepared to wait the ten to thirty minutes which seemed to comprise most women's concept of 'a moment'. But almost instantly, the lights on the upper floor shut off and she came down the stairs, her midi-length skirt rippling and flowing above a pair of delicately blinged flats.

A deep red scarf matching the background of the tribal print fabric in her dress was tied in a triangle overtop of a jean jacket. Her folded hair was clipped to the back of her head with a large barrette.

41

He was staring at her so hard she looked at him with some concern. "Are you okay?"

He realized he had actually been holding his breath. He responded with a shy grin. "Sorry, beautiful women tend to have that effect on me. Ready?"

At the truck, Mya bent over to gather up her long skirt to climb in. Colton stopped her. "Turn around and face me," he said. "Duck your head." Placing his hands on her waist, he lifted her into the seat. He made sure the material of her skirt was inside the cab before closing the door.

When they walked into the club, Duncan was standing at the cover charge table. Upon seeing them, he wagged a finger warningly in Mya's face. "Don't do it, girl. I swear I'll have you banned if you use any name but Cool Train tonight." She scrunched up her face and stuck out her tongue at him as he shook Colton's hand. "So tonight, your drinks are on me as a consolation prize for not being able to find a better date than my little sister."

"Little sister? We're the same age."

"Yeah, you're still a foot shorter. Come on I'll show you to your table." He put his large hand on Mya's shoulder and maneuvered them across the room. He ended at a small table near the stage. "Do not cause trouble," he said as he tapped his finger on the end of her nose, "or I'll tell Mom."

After seating Mya, Colton headed to the bar to get their beers. Waiting his turn, he watched Mya as she looked around the room with quiet interest. He spotted a couple of males who assumed she was there by herself. They were posturing within her line of vision, attempting to gain her attention. Her eyes slid over them as though they were holes in the growing crowd.

When he returned, the warmth in her smile seemed to light up their table even as the lights dimmed indicating the start of the music.

The temperature in the club was rising in direct relation to the number of bodies pushing into it. Mya untied the scarf around her neck, sliding it into the sleeve of her jean jacket as she slipped it off her shoulders. Colton's eyes were drawn to the curve of her breasts the V-neckline of her dress revealed. By clubbing standards, it was extremely modest which had the effect of making it feel incredibly provocative.

Cool Train kicked off the show and the music began. At the end of the first set, he announced he was going to slow it down and the last song was being dedicated to one particular couple. He pointed directly at their table and motioning them to the dance floor.

Taking her hand, Colton pulled Mya after him. When Joe Cocker started singing *You Are So Beautiful*, he pulled her in tight with one arm while cupping her other hand against his chest. She let her forehead rest in the crook of his neck, relishing the feel of his arms.

As they moved in slow rhythm to the song, they were unaware eyes were watching closely. "Shit, he's in love or damn close to it," his mother said as she watched a blissed-out look settle on her son's face as soon as he had taken her in his arms… whoever 'her' was.

She held up her cell phone and waited until the music stopped, then snapped a picture of the girl's face when she stepped away from Colton. Studying the image, she had the distinct feeling she should know this person, but couldn't quite figure out why or where. Leaning over, Wanda Williams showed it to her friend, Babs. "She looks familiar, but I don't know why."

Babs took the phone and studied it before handing it back. "Got me, but I agree she does kinda look like I've seen her before."

"Well, we're gonna have to figure out exactly who she is," Wanda said grimly, continuing to stare at the image on her phone.

"Can we at least do it at your house? I am way too old for the club scene."

The two women finished swallowing the contents of their drinks before making their way through the crowd toward the exit and Wanda's house.

Babs sat on the couch and kicked off her shoes; putting her feet up on the coffee table with a happy sigh as Wanda returned from the kitchen, handing her a wine cooler before carrying her own beer to her recliner. "Okay, so this whole espionage trip tonight was just so you could get a look at the broad Colton currently has the hots for? Wanda, he is twenty-nine, almost thirty. He's old enough to pick his own partners."

"But I don't know anything about her. He sees her and tells me nothing. I don't even know her name."

43

"I assume you've gone through his cell phone," Babs asked drily.

"Of course, I have. According to it, she doesn't exist. No name, no number, no pictures... nothing."

"My advice is leave it alone. If Colton is getting serious about this girl, it would not be a good time to interfere. It might come across as some kind of competition requiring him to choose between her and you. That may not work in your favor."

"Of course, it would. I'll always be his number one girl."

*****

The drive back from the club was quiet. It felt refreshing after the intense noise of the crowd and the music. He realized she had the rare ability to remain silent without it feeling awkward.

When he shut off the truck, he touched her arm. "Wait." Coming around to the passenger side, he opened the door, and lifted her to the ground. He kept his hand on her back as they made their way to her door where he let go, holding out his hand for her key.

"So what are you doing tomorrow?" he asked.

"Tomorrow is the baby shower Nancy and I are putting on for Anita."

"Do you need a ride?"

"Thank you. That is kind, but Nancy is picking me up."

"Then I guess I'll see you later," he said. Placing his fingers under her chin, he tilted her face up. She did not pull away as he lowered his head to gently press his lips against hers. Raising up, he watched as she slowly opened her eyes. For a moment, something fragile floated in them. Then she smiled and stepped back. "Thank you, Colton, for the loveliest time I've had in ages."

He pulled the key out and handed it to her. Although a part of him was hoping she would invite him in, another recognized he would be disappointed if she did. One of her attractions lay in not doing what everyone else did.

She stepped inside and closed the door. He waited until he heard the lock engage before heading to his truck.

*****

Wanda was surprised when she heard Colton's key in the door. She glanced at her cell phone sitting beside her and realized it wasn't even midnight. She had assumed by the look on his face at the club he probably wouldn't be coming home tonight.

"So how was your evening?" she asked, watching him closely.

"It was good," he answered as he headed to his bedroom. In a few minutes, he was back wearing a pair of sleep pants and one of his old Henleys.

He dropped on the couch and pointed to the television. "What are you watching?"

"I have no idea. When I dozed off, it was some dumb romance movie about…" She was cut off by a godawful yowl and Cinnamon stalked into the room. She sat down beside Colton, fixing her eyes on him and yowled again.

"I just got home, girl" he said to the cat, who immediately yowled a reply. "I have just been told it's bedtime. 'Night," he said scooping up his cat and slinging her over his shoulder.

His mom stared unseeingly at the TV trying to puzzle out what was happening. His noncommittal 'good" was not jibing with his expression when she watched him dance. Either something had gone south after she and Babs had left, or she had read a whole lot more into the dance than was really there. Apparently the girl didn't matter much after all. She breathed a sigh of relief and clicked off the television.

In his bedroom, Colton lifted his comforter so Cinnamon could crawl under and curl up on his shoulder. "I love you, Cin, but I really wish another blue-eyed beauty was lying on my shoulder," he whispered.

Chapter 7

Mya picked up the carefully wrapped quilted wall hanging when she heard a car honking. Nancy's SUV waited at the curb while Mya locked her door and dashed through the rain drops. She put the gift in the backseat, and then climbed in.

"Okay, I want every single detail, especially the juicy details, about him," Nancy said.

"Who him?"

Nancy glanced at her, "Don't play dumb, girl. You know 'who him'. The tall, dark, and extremely handsome man you have been spotted with at the flea market and the Caverns."

"Duncan blabbed."

"You bet Duncan blabbed. Come on, we all know you from way back and your very convenient way of forgetting to mention important stuff."

Mya squirmed a little. "I know you are my best friend ever and we have shared everything since we were in first grade, but I feel like if I actually talk about him, he will turn out to just be an illusion fabricated by my overactive imagination."

"And underutilized libido?"

Nancy glanced at Mya when she got no response to the old joke between them. She had the very neutral expression she wore when something was affecting her deeply. Nancy looked back at the road thoughtfully. Was Mya finally falling in love?

Chapter 8

"So what are your plans today," Wanda asked when Colton wandered out of his bedroom in search of coffee.

He shrugged. "The usual—laundry, garbage; maybe see if I can get the grass cut if we get a break in the weather."

Although she watched carefully, Colton's expression gave her no clue to what might be going on in his head as he picked up his coffee and went back to his bedroom to dress.

Seemingly driven by a nervous energy, Colton moved from task to task, not stopping until it was nearly four p.m. Wanda found it interesting he had not once picked up his cell phone to check for messages or texts. He obviously wasn't expecting to hear from anyone.

In fact, it was her phone which beeped with an incoming message. "Hey, Lindsay said they just made a batch of chicken and jojos if you want to run down, and pick up dinner," she said.

Colton disappeared into his room, emerging in his jean jacket and tucking his wallet into his back pocket as he crossed to the door.

"Don't forget the ranch," his mom called after him.

The Deuces parking lot was amazingly empty when he pulled in. Inside, Lindsay placed a bag with the chicken and jojos on the counter.

"The ranch is already in there," she said. "And congratulation on hitting the date jackpot."

Colton looked at her questioningly. "What?"

"Mya Parker as in 'Parker Premier Properties' Parker, that's who you were with last night at the Caverns, right? My husband and I had a night out and we saw you dancing."

49

"How do you know Mya?"

"We were in the same class at high school, although she mainly hung out with the rest of the Quail Crest kids."

"Quail Crest kids?"

"You know, the kids who actually lived up on Quail Crest. They had, like, their own clique."

"Are you sure it's the same person?"

Lindsay lowered her head and rolled her eyes up, looking at him like he was a moron. "How many people do you know have that color of eyes and are named Mya? It's her, trust me."

Colton was grateful when the conversation was interrupted by a couple setting a case of beer on the counter. Lifting a hand to Lindsay, he dragged the bag with the chicken off the counter and headed home.

Quail Crest kept repeating in his brain. Although it had recently given up its preeminence in being the town's upper class bastion to the newer development over by the golf course, it still was recognized as a solid high-end neighborhood.

And Mya had grown up there. And she was Jack Parker's daughter. Half the construction projects he had worked on were Parker projects.

By the time he reached home, a toxic brew of emotions was rising in him. Anger, and the sting of inferiority began to filter his thoughts. He was angry with Mya for not telling him her origins, and instead filling him with stories of her purported handmade life. The inferiority of those who grow up poor when in the presence of people who teethed on the proverbial silver spoon made its weight known as well.

He had been totally enchanted by her uniqueness. She had been filling his thoughts every second of every day since he walked into her gallery and found those amazing blue eyes looking up at him. He had even begun to fantasize about a day when he might wake up beside her.

And now she turned out to be friggin' Jack Parker's daughter; a rich girl getting her kicks slumming with a construction worker from the wrong side of Reigl Street.

His mother watched him as he picked off bits of chicken and fed them to Cinnamon, barely taking any for himself.

"Something wrong, kid?" she asked.

He answered by giving an irritated shrug of his shoulders. Picking upon his plate, he disappeared into the kitchen before slamming into his bedroom.

Even after he went to bed, his head buzzed causing him to toss and turn until Cinnamon hissed at him and demanded to be let out.

Chapter 9

The shower for Anita had proven to be an immense success on many levels. Not only was the impending Miss Penelope Dunwoody outfitted with everything a newborn could want, Mya had gotten three commissions for other wall hangings from the women present based on the hanging she had created.

The first few days of the week found her scheduling in six windows businesses wanting to transition to spring/summer themes. And Nancy's husband, Wally, called her to let her know he had finally secured all the funding/donations needed to convert the empty dime store building over on Henderson into a youth center. She promised she would bid to paint various walls with appropriate graphics for the different age groups he wanted the center to serve. Additionally, one of the women at the shower had stopped by the gallery and purchased one of her paintings. Her bank account felt a little less strained.

While her professional life burgeoned, her private life was increasingly bleak. She had waited every evening for the sound of her door opening and Colton to come through it. She had even deliberately left her open sign on later than usual. When the following weekend had come and gone, she acknowledged his final 'see you later' was, in fact, 'see you never.'

She found herself in the exact place she had long ago promised herself she would never again enter; the place where she let someone get in enough to hurt her. If she let herself think about him, her chest got tight, making it hard for her to breathe. She didn't blame him; she blamed herself for not being quite good enough for him.

It was the recurrent theme of her life. She was the imbecile and she deserved the misery she was currently swimming in.

She bent her head to her work. If she worked hard enough; long enough each day, she could drive the memory of his kiss, arms, and touch into a back corner of her mind where it would eventually drop into a file labeled "Another Thing I Don't Deserve."

*****

Colton had always been able to turn off his interest in women like flicking a light switch. He was interested, and then he wasn't. He assumed it would be the same with Mya, but the damn light would barely dim. The first week, he had found his truck heading in the direction of her gallery instead of home after work. He had forced himself to keep driving rather than pull in.

The second and third week didn't get easier. The sight of long hair, a certain shade of blue, a flowing skirt and thoughts of Mya immediately consumed him. There was a low level longing gnawing constantly at his midsection.

Chapter 10

The beginning of the fourth week found the construction crew meeting at the old dime store building to start a new project. Although most of them arrived promptly at eight a.m., the contractor told them not to start work on the demolition yet. Apparently, there was going to be some press event to capture a picture of the first sledgehammer swing to promote the future youth center set to rise out of the dust of the old building.

Standing around, the guys commented on the good fortune of having a Starbucks located right across the street. As they were eyeing the establishment, the door opened and Colton caught his breath when Mya stepped out followed by a big blonde man who had the physique of a linebacker.

'Oh, baby, come to Papa," one of the men said. He fist bumped another of the men when they saw she was, indeed, crossing the street.

At the sidewalk, she stopped and reached into the kangaroo pocket on her purple hoodie sweater, bringing out her cell phone. The man continued in their direction, stopping to shake hands with the contractor. He was then introduced as Wally Bergstrom, who, with his wife Nancy, was the force behind the creation of the center.

Colton flicked through his memory... he had definitely heard the name before from Mya. Closing his eyes momentarily, he connected it with the bone boxes. Nancy was her counselor friend.

Still covertly watching her, he felt something loom large behind him. In a moment, Duncan circled the group and was bro shaking Wally's hand. It made him feel awkward since Duncan knew he had spent time with Mya. Colton wondered if she had told Duncan about the disappearing act he pulled.

Mya completed her texting and was heading in their direction when a Mercedes Benz S-Class sedan pulled smoothly into the curb.

Mya stopped, her body going defensively rigid.

Colton watched curiously. There was only one person who drove such an expensive car in town— Mya's dad.

Jack Parker stepped out of the car wearing an impeccable grey suit over a white polo shirt. Although the day was overcast, he had sunglasses on. He pulled them off as he circled the front of the car to open the passenger door. A young woman stepped out attired in a short tight dress with plenty of bust pushing out of the top of it. She clutched at his arm as she balanced on the thin stiletto heels of her shoes. She didn't look much older than Mya.

Looking around, the man apparently noticed the woman standing on the sidewalk was his daughter.

Dragging the young woman along, he strode to her. Like Duncan, he was well over six feet so he loomed over Mya when he stopped in front of her. She didn't appear to be intimidated by it.

"Mya," he boomed. "Damn, what's it been a couple of years?"

Mya crossed her arms over her chest and eyed him coldly. "More like four years, Dad."

"Really? I wouldn't have guessed it," he said as he apparently gave the information about a nanosecond of thought. "So, Mya, I would like you to meet..."

"I know. Your flavor of the week."

The two women exchanged hostile looks.

"So what have you been up to? Found something useful to do with your life or are you still into finger painting?"

Mya flinched before quietly saying. "No, Dad, I'm still the big disappointment I've always been."

But her dad had already disengaged from the conversation and was looking past her at people who were coming down the sidewalk in their direction. Turning slightly, he called to Wally. "Hey, the press is here. Let's do this." He moved past his daughter as if she had suddenly ceased to exist.

"What an asshole," Colton heard one of the men whisper. He looked from the back of the retreating man to Mya. Her expression had the forlornness of an abandoned child. All his conjectures about her life broke apart leaving a foul taste in his mind with their wrongness.

Followed by television and print reporters, Jack led the charge back to the door of the building, his girlfriend trailing the pack. The crew stepped back as the group pushed through the door into the building. Jack stopped long enough to grab the girl by her shoulder.

"Best you stay out here, Brittany. Don't want to get dust all over your pretty dress," he said as he disappeared inside.

She stood tapping the toe of her high-heeled shoe in irritation at being excluded before looking over the men who were goggling her attractions with smirks and winks at each other. Her look of pouty boredom at their appreciation switched to a silken smile when her eyes lighted on Colton.

She opened her tiny clutch and pulled out a card, then asked one of the men for a pen. He was practically drooling into her cleavage as he handed it over. She scribbled something on the card. She handed off the pen as she headed directly to Colton, pushing deep into his personal space.

She held the card up so he could see there was a telephone number written on the back. "I think you know what to do with this," she purred as she leaned in and pushed it into his jean pocket. "And I definitely think you know what to do with that," she added, staring directly at his crotch.

He flushed and stepped back, acutely uncomfortable. He anxiously looked past her to where Mya had been standing. He had already screwed up things with her, but he didn't want to add to his sins by appearing to be hustling another woman in front of her.

She was nowhere to be seen.

There was noise at the door, and, following a mass exit, everyone disappeared except Wally. Blowing out a relieved breath, he nodded to the contractor.

"Okay, men, let's take 'er down."

Sliding a respirator over his face, Colton pulled his baseball cap out of his back pocket and put it on. He grabbed one of the sledgehammers leaning against the wall and followed. Just before he stepped into the building, he pulled Brittany's card out of his pocket, flicking it on the ground.

At noon, most of the men went off to purchase their lunches. Colton grabbed his lunch sack and bottle of Gatorade out of his truck and headed to the back end of the building where the first delivery of lumber provided seating.

He had just bitten into leftover cold chicken when Duncan wandered in carrying a Subway bag. He pointed to the space next to Colton. "Mind?" he asked.

Colton gestured toward the spot on the lumber. Duncan sat and pulled a foot long sandwich out of the bag. Unwrapping it, he took a healthy bite.

Colton looked back at the chicken thigh he was holding, wondering if Duncan was going to say anything about his blowing off Mya.

"You ever meet Jack Parker before today?"

Colton shook his head. "No. I've worked on plenty of his projects though."

"I've known him most of my life and believe me he is a piece of work. He lives for the real estate deal, golf, and satisfying his dick. Pretty much in that order."

"And Mya?"

"Dude, you saw today. Did it look like Jack even remembered he has a daughter?"

"What about her mom?"

"Apparently her mother died before Mya was even a year old. And what he showed up with today is what he has always brought home, so not much chance of any of them even being remotely interested in his kid. Luckily, she had Nancy's mom, Sharon, and my mom to fill in as best they could. We pretty much raised her between our two families."

Duncan shoved another bite of the sandwich in his mouth, washing it down with his drink, as he looked down the long hall of memory.

"Mya couldn't have been more than six when she and Jack moved into the house across from Sharon, just two houses over from our place. They had only been there a few months when Sharon's doorbell rang about nine o'clock one night. It was one of those dark, cold, pouring rain nights.

"When Sharon opened the door, there was this little girl with one hand wrapped in a bloody washcloth, and some change in the other. She asked very politely if Sharon might have a Band-Aid she could buy.

"Both my mom and Sharon are nurses over at Trinity Hospital so Sharon immediately examined Mya's hand and realized she actually needed stitches. Apparently she had cut herself deeply trying to carve off a hunk of cheese for dinner. And yeah, for the record, Jack was not home; nobody was home. Just this little kid foraging like a small animal for something to eat.

"My mom was on duty that night when Sharon brought Mya in. Between the two of them, they were able to get the doctor to suture her up without actually providing parental permission. The thing which got to Sharon and my mom was Mya never cried or fussed. Just sat there like a little soldier and took it. And if you've ever had stitches put in, you know it hurts like hell, at least when they are using the needle to numb everything."

He suddenly chuckled to himself. "When we were all working on Mya's gallery, Eric sliced himself with a drywall cutter and had to have like two stitches. I thought they were going to have to give him general anesthesia to get it done."

Colton looked at him. "So she really did renovate the place with you and her other friends?"

Duncan looked back. "Damn straight she did. I wired the whole thing for her, and, even though she is family, she insisted on paying me; and not just a token amount, the same amount as if I was doing a regular job for someone else. I tried to make her give me less, but she wouldn't hear of it. She can be really stubborn about doing what she thinks is right. If she had done what I wanted, she wouldn't have ended up having to sell her car to finish it."

Colton stared at the dusty floor while Duncan studied him.

"You think Mya was feeding you some kind of crock of shit, don't you."

Colton's expression went from pensive to embarrassed.

Duncan's voice dropped to an even lower octave. "I'm gonna tell you something. Mya doesn't lie. Mya doesn't cry. And she would hack off her right arm and give it to you if she thought you needed it.

"What she isn't is a cock tease, party girl, or easy lay. If that's what you're looking for, well, you have Brittany's phone number."

With one last hard look at Colton, Duncan stood up and pitched his crushed sack in a steel drum.

Colton put his unfinished chicken back in his lunch. He felt like a total prick.

He drove passed the gallery after work. The downstairs was un-lit. He idled for a few moments in front wondering if he should try the door anyway. Then he asked himself for what? He had no good explanation for just vanishing, and, odds were, Mya wouldn't be much interested in how his convoluted thinking had somehow turned her into the bad guy.

He put his foot on the accelerator and drove away. He was still trying to convince himself he didn't need her, but he knew she sure as hell didn't need someone like him.

Chapter 11

By the second week in May, a lot of the framing had been completed at the future youth center; enough it was possible to recognize the configuration of rooms and the flow of future traffic.

Colton had just carried in a couple of two by fours and set them down when Wally came in through a future door with Mya. She was busy watching the sketchbook her pencil was moving over.

"Careful," Colton said as they approached the lumber on the floor.

When she looked at him, the sight of those blue eyes slammed into his chest with the force of a fist. "Thank you," was all she said. There was no accusation, or recrimination in her expression. In fact, there was nothing indicating they had ever met before this moment other than a trace of sadness drifting in her eyes.

She stepped over the boards and moved along with Wally. Colton didn't see her hand shaking or know she was struggling to breathe.

They had disappeared when Duncan came through the door carrying a roll of electrical wire over his shoulder. He was followed by another crew member, who was busy looking back the way he had just come. "Wow, would I love to get me a piece of that," the guy said as he jerked his thumb in the direction Mya and Wally had gone.

Colton found his hands balling into fists. But it was Duncan's large hand grabbing the front of the man's tee-shirt, pulling him up till he had to stand on tiptoe.

"Let's get one thing straight, asswipe. She is my sister," Duncan said.

The guy made a face, "Yeah, right, she's your sister. Sorry, man, but you and her ain't exactly the same color."

61

Duncan lifted him a few inches higher so his toes were scrambling to find purchase. "Trust me, she is family, and, as such, you will never lay a hand or a filthy thought on her ever or I will break you in two. Got it?"

He lowered the man down as Wally and Mya came back into the area. Mya threw herself at Duncan. "Pictures!"

Duncan pulled out his cell phone, poking icons until be brought up some images before handing the phone to Mya.

"Oh, look, Wally." When she held the phone out to the man, the crew member caught a glimpse of a tiny black baby nestled in someone's arms.

She swiped through the rest with an adoring expression before handing the phone back. "I have the most beautiful niece in the world. You done good, bro," she said as she stood on her toes to kiss Duncan's cheek.

"Yeah, and between you, Shonda, and Monique, she is going to be the most spoiled brat in the world, too."

"No, that would have been you."

"Go away. I'm on the clock and Wally is gonna start docking me."

As Wally and Mya left, the man looked at Duncan. "Sorry, man, my bad."

*****

Mya refused Wally's offer to take her home and instead opted for the bus. She had come close to betraying herself when she saw Colton, although it was evident from his indifferent look seeing her was meaningless to him. But it had dragged back to the forefront the memories she had been working to push out of her consciousness.

She stared out the window. "He doesn't want you. He's moved on so quit with the unrequited bullshit. You need to work—just work. That's your life. Remember, it's your mission to become a renowned finger painter."

Oddly enough, as she walked from the bus stop home, she recognized seeing Colton and acknowledging he had truly lost interest was actually working to help steady her. She put her key in the lock at the gallery, then just looked at it. He was never going to come through the door again; time to smudge the ghosts away. She turned the key.

*****

Coming through his own front door, Colton, headed to the kitchen for a beer before shutting himself in his bedroom. Sitting on the edge of the bed, he stared at the bottle he was holding loosely in his hands. Hearing a paw at the door, he got up to open it. Cinnamon serpentined her way around the door before lofting herself onto the bed.

Colton looked at her. "You sure you want to keep hanging out with a friggin' asshole, Cin? Yeah, that would totally be me. An idiot who threw away any chance he might have had with what may be the most amazing person he has ever met. They don't come any dumber."

Cin answered with a soft yowl and rubbed against him arm. He reached out to tickle the top of her head. "Thanks, girl, but you judge people by their ability to use the can opener. Those are pretty low standards even I can meet." He let his hand drop back into his lap. His world felt darker and smaller than it had any time since his dad offed himself.

Chapter 12

The following week the weather took a turn sending the temperatures into the nineties. By Friday, even with the industrial grade fans Wally had delivered, the interior of the building was unbearable. The construction crew was sent home by 3:30 p.m.

Colton decided to swing by Deuces to pick up drinks for the next week's work. As he swung into the parking lot through the east driveway, he saw the ambulance parked by the south end of the building. Stepping out of his truck, he caught sight of a couple of navy blue shirts leaning over someone; an opened medical kit, sitting next to them. Probably one of the town's drunks had passed out again. It was a relatively common event at the only place with available booze three hundred and sixty five days a year.

He pulled open the store's door and circled back to the cooler grabbing an eight pack of Gatorade, and a six pack each of water, and beer. He got in line behind a woman who was paying for a couple of packs of cigarettes.

"Do you think she's going to be alright?" the woman was asking his mother as she handed over her money. His mom answered with a disinterested shrug.

"Don't know."

Colton swung his purchases up on the counter. "What's going on?" he asked as he dug in his pocket, pulling out a twenty dollar bill.

"Oh, the gal that paints our window passed out."

Colton stared at his mom for a moment before he shot out the door.

"Shit," his mother said. Now she knew why Colton's date looked familiar.

65

Colton crossed swiftly to squat beside the paramedics. It was Mya who lay against one of the men's shoulder. "What's wrong with her?" he asked staring at her very flushed face.

"Too much heat. You know her?"

"Yes. She's Mya Parker, a..." He hesitated. "A friend."

"Look, she's kinda borderline in needing to be hospitalized, but if you know someone who could get her home and take care her for the next twelve to twenty-four hours, we won't transport."

"Let me get my truck."

Standing up, he turned and almost ran into Lindsay. "Your mom wants me to get the ladder Mya was using. It belongs to the store."

Looking back, Colton saw a four foot ladder beside a large canvas tote. He handed it off to Lindsay before picking up the tote and sprinting to his truck. He slung the bag into the bed. As he opened the door and stepped up, his mom came out of the store with his purchases. She opened the passenger door and placed them on the seat.

"So what do you want me to bring home for dinner tonight?"

"I won't be home," he said as he dropped in the seat and fired up the truck.

He pulled up just beyond the nose of the ambulance. Jumping out, he opened the passenger door, slinging the items from the seat into the truck bed.

"Air conditioner on?" one of the paramedics asked as they lifted Mya to her feet; using the fireman's carry to get her to and into the truck. They got her seated, and secured the seatbelt across her. The paramedic waved his hand in front of the cold air blasting out and then adjusted the vent slightly so it was blowing directly on her before shutting the door.

The other was scribbling information on a sheet of paper. "Okay, get her cooled down. Fans, air conditioning, iced towels or bath, whatever you have. Make sure she drinks plenty of fluids. I'd like to see at least a quart of fluids in her over the next couple of hours. She's going to be totally wiped out so she'll probably want to sleep. Watch her closely. She starts vomiting, gets really mentally confused, or loses consciousness again, call us ASAP because she'll need to be hospitalized. Any questions?"

Colton shook his head as the man handed him the paper. Getting back into the truck, he looked over at Mya. Her breathing was fast and shallow. He reached out to touch her hand. "I'm taking you home, Mya."

He maneuvered the truck out the south drive and pointed it in the direction of the other side of town. With an effort, Mya pushed the seatbelt harness off and behind her right shoulder before lying over in the seat; the top of her head pressed against his thigh. Her braid draped over her limp hands.

Although it probably did not take him any longer to get from Deuces to the front of her gallery than normal, it felt much longer. She never made a sound; just lay deathly still with her eyes closed even after he parked and got out of the truck.

Opening the passenger door, Colton touched her shoulder. "Mya, where is your key?"

She tried to reach in the pocket of her cutoffs, but even that minimal effort seemed too much. Colton slid his fingers in and felt the small skull of her Day of the Dead keychain. Slipping it out, he reached in the truck bed and pulled out her tote, sliding the handle over his shoulder. He then grabbed the water, Gatorade and six pack; balancing everything as he went to open the door.

When the door was open, and everything dumped on the counter, he leaped down the stairs and back to the truck.

"Let's get you inside," he said as he carefully used her arm to pull her to a sitting position. Unlatching the seatbelt, he slid his hand under her legs, swinging them in his direction. Moving in close, he lifted her down. She leaned into him while he held her steady.

"Ready?"

He wrapped one arm around her waist. She clutched for his other hand as they headed to the gallery. She relied on his strength to get her up the stairs. Once inside, Colton kicked the door closed.

"Is your bedroom upstairs?"

Her "yes" was a wispy exhale of air.

He carefully guided her up the stairs. They had just stepped onto the second floor when her legs gave. He swung her up into his arms. He could feel the heat still pouring off her body.

Spying what looked like corner of a bed to the right, he carried her towards it. Setting her on it, he undid the buttons on the shirt she was wearing, pushing it off her shoulders to reveal a flowered camisole top. He pulled her canvas slip-ons off her feet. Then wrapping his arms around her shoulders and under her knees, Colton laid her on the bed, tugging a pillow beneath her head. Her eyes closed instantly.

A fan sat across the room in a retro metal patio chair. He circled the bed and turned it on, positioning it so it blew directly across her bare shoulders and legs.

Fluids. She needed fluids. He headed back to the main floor. He carried the water, Gatorade, and beer to the kitchen. Opening the refrigerator, he was startled to see there was already beer in it before remembering he had left it weeks ago. He was not surprised to see there was almost no food. He put the water in after pulling one of the bottles out of the plastic rings. Back upstairs, he sat on the edge of the bed. He lifted Mya up, allowing her weight to rest against him. "You have to drink," he said softly as he held the bottle to her lips. She sipped the water until about a quarter of the bottle was gone before turning her head away.

He laid her back down. She rolled on her side away from him. He touched her face, bare shoulder and leg with the back of his fingers. Although still warm, her skin was no longer blazing. Her breathing was beginning to slow as well.

He relaxed enough to look around the room. He realized the bed he was sitting on was suspended from the ceiling by four large chains attached to a platform. Iridescent colors played off the blue-black chains like oil on water. Silver garlands of tiny moons and stars were woven through them. The wooden platform was painted the blue violet of a sunrise sky.

There was a floating shelf on either side of the bed with matching industrial looking reading lights. Directly above the bed was a large skylight, washing the room in light.

An old fashion double hung window was offset above a long storage unit running the length of the end of the room. A retro reproduction record player sat on top while dozens of records albums were store below. Books and art pieces were dotted over the rest.

He carefully stood up. There were two doors in the bedroom. One opened into a vintage inspired bath complete with a claw-foot tub. The other was a meticulously organized walk-in closet with built in dressers and a shoe rack.

He wandered out into the main area of the upstairs. Wide counters with storage underneath ran the perimeter of the space dominating the second floor. There appeared to be separate stations for her painting, weaving, and quilting. The wall adjacent to the bedroom had floor-to-ceiling shelving units filled with color-coded fabric and yarn. In the center of the space at the top of the stairs was a huge worktable scattered over with large sheets of drawing paper. Pint mason jars were filled with colored pencils, felt pens, and drawing pencils. Like the downstairs, everything was immaculate and well organized.

He crossed back into the bedroom and sat on the edge of the bed, watching her. Normal color had crept back into her face and her skin where he touched it was cool. He saw her slowly opening her eyes. She rolled onto her back and looked up at him.

"Colton?" she whispered.

Looking into her blue eyes, he found he was desperate to get her back in his arms. He reached for the water bottle he had left sitting on the floor, holding it where she could see it.

"Yes, please," her voice barely audible as she held out her hand for it. He slipped his arm under her shoulders and supplied the lift to help her into a sitting position before putting the bottle in her hand. He wrapped his hand around hers, and shifted so she was supported by his body. This time she drank the rest of the bottle. When she finished, she slipped her hand out from under his, but made no move away from him.

She could feel his heart beat against her back and his breath in her hair; smell the construction dust and sweat on him. She didn't want to move for fear if she did he would dissolve into nothing but another mirage haunting her heart.

She couldn't remember how he ended up in her bedroom, or if he was actually there. "Is this a dream?" she murmured.

"If it is, is it a good dream or a bad one?" he whispered in her ear.

She was quiet for a long minute. "It depends on how it ends."

She began to drift back into sleep, her body relaxing into him.

He lay down on the bed, letting her body slip off his. She turned her head in his direction so her face was only inches from his.

He raised up, resting his head in his hand as he studied her; the fan of dark lashes, the short straight nose, and those lips calling to his every time he saw her. He reached out and carefully slid her fallen camisole strap back over her bare shoulder. He noticed the cami had twisted, revealing a few inches of slender waist above the top of her cutoffs. He stared at it becoming aware of just how vulnerable she was right now; all her defenses muted.

Images of the jerk at the construction site, the guy at the flea market who had run into her, and the guys who looked like they were mentally undressing her at the club surged into his consciousness. His own blood began to heat as he mentally engaged them in battle. The mere thought of some other man putting his hands on her shot rage through him. Then it hit him like a two by four to the back of his skull. As it permeated his brain, he actually felt disoriented.

He carefully slipped off the bed and headed downstairs. In the kitchen, he pulled a beer out of the refrigerator. Setting it on the counter, he twisted the top off. Abruptly, he put his hands on the edge, leaning into them as his head dropped down.

Now he understood why he couldn't flick her off. He was in love with Mya.

He turned around and looked. He didn't want to be anywhere but right here. He didn't want to touch anyone but her. He wanted her to go to sleep in his arms and wake up to those amazing eyes every day. He wanted to feed her when she forgot to eat and watch over her when she couldn't defend herself. He wanted to catch her every time she fell.

Grabbing his beer off the counter, he went to sit on the steps to the upstairs. Everything in his life shifted. What he wanted more than anything he had ever wanted was lying on the bed upstairs. And his jackass actions had probably pushed her out of his reach forever.

*****

Upstairs, Mya rolled onto her back and opened her eyes. She moved her hand across the side of the bed. There was no one there. She closed her eyes. It had been a dream... a strange convoluted dream of heat that somehow transported her from Deuces to her own bed. Lost inside it, she had felt Colton. Felt him so strongly she could still summon up the sensation of his arms around her; laying against his chest; feeling his heartbeat behind hers. But, in fact, the only heartbeat she actually could feel was her own echoing off the bed.

She pushed herself to a sitting position, turning so she could look out the window on the far wall. Pulling her hair over her shoulder, she slipped the elastic off the end and unbraided it. She should get her hairbrush but she felt completely enervated, like she had just come through a bad illness. Instead, she raked her fingers through it, spilling it over her shoulder and down her front to rest in her lap and on the bed beside her. It rippled as the air from the fan caught it.

"Mya?"

She went very still before turning her head slightly in the direction of his voice. "What is happening?" she asked quietly. "Everything is melted together in my head. Real is all mixed up with strange things."

Colton walked around the bed and squatted down in front of her. "You collapsed at Deuces from the heat. You've been pretty trashed the last couple of hours."

"You brought me home?"

"Yes." He twisted the top off the water bottle he had brought upstairs and handed it to her. "You need to drink some more."

He could still feel the slight tremor in her hands as he put the bottle into them. She lifted it and he was gratified to see she took a long swallow of it.

"I want you to try to finish it all, and, if you think you will be alright for a little bit, I am going to go home and clean up."

A flash of inevitability crossed her face. She managed the faintest of smiles. "I will be fine. Thank you for what you have done, but there's no need for you screw up the rest of your Friday night by coming back."

"I am coming back," he said firmly. "Someone is supposed to keep an eye on you for the next twenty-four hours according to the paramedics who treated you at Deuces."

Disbelief of his words was clear in her eyes as she looked at him.

He stood up, and touched the bottle. "Keep drinking. I want to see it all gone by the time I'm back."

Downstairs, he dug in his pocket and pulled out her key, locking the door. Heading to his truck, he kept it clutched in his hand like a talisman.

His mom wasn't home when he pulled in. He hurried to his bedroom and stripped out of his clothes, kicking them into the pile in the corner. He showered and dressed in fresh jeans and tee-shirt. Cinnamon sat on the bed as he pulled an old backpack out of his closet and stuffed it with changes of clothes; enough to take him to Monday. He added his kit before zipping it up. He carefully tucked Mya's key in his pocket.

He stopped to scratch Cinnamon. "Sorry, babe, but you're gonna have to fly solo this weekend. If you get bored, you can do some laundry," he said acknowledging the mound. "I'll be back." At least, his cat looked like she believed he would return.

He pondered food choices as he headed to the grocery store. He was pretty sure Mya was probably not up to pizza or nacho tonight.

*****

Mya finished the bottle of water. The rehydration helped clear the haziness from her brain and lift her energy level enough she figured she could handle a shower to wash away the gritty-feeling dried sweat.

Her hair and body wrapped in towels, she stood in her closet debating whether to actually get dressed or just slip into her nightwear. When she realized it was a bigger decision than she could make, she reached for the boy's boxer shorts and oversized tee-shirt she usually slept in.

She returned to sit on the bed in front of the fan as she combed out her wet hair, letting the moving air draw the moisture from it as she mindlessly ran the comb through it over and over.

She tried to sort through the events of this afternoon, isolating what had actually happened out of the chaos of the bits and pieces orbiting just beyond clarity. Somehow she had been gifted with a few hours of Colton back in her life, but it was deeply shaded by her physical debilitation.

She understood what she was trying to do was stupid. Why was she hunting for memories she would just end up trying to bury along with the previous ones? She didn't know how or why Colton ended up being the one to bring her home and look after her, but now the event was over and he was gone. She didn't want to deal with a repeat of the pain that had sprung in the wake of his vanishing act.

"Please don't come back, Colton… ever," she whispered.

Chapter 13

Colton's progress through the store was slower than he had planned as he considered whether each item he put in the cart would appeal to Mya. He decided scrambled eggs with toast would make a good dinner, along with vanilla ice cream and fresh strawberries. He added some bottled teas to chill along with bagels, fruit-infused cream cheese, and fruit spreads. He was studying the lunch meats when someone banged into his cart. It was his mother.

"Hey, I'm doing the shopping," she said, "because you said you wouldn't be home."

"I'm not going to be home."

She looked over what was in his cart. "What the hell are you buying? We don't eat that."

"I'm not shopping for us."

"You're shopping for her?" There was derision in his mother's voice.

Colton's dark eyes flashed as he looked at his mother. "She has a name. It's Mya."

"I know her name and I know who she is."

Colton dropped a package of turkey in the cart, then backed it up and headed around his mother toward the check-out.

As she watched his tall, broad-shouldered frame stride away, she remembered a shorter, skinnier thirteen-year-old who had stood beside her at Johnny's funeral and took her hand. "Don't worry, Mom, I won't leave you ever, I promise." It was a promise no outsider was going make him break.

It was the time of year when the days were long and light, so, although the clock was leaning on eight when he pulled back in front of Mya's gallery, shadows were just forming. He carried the three bags of groceries he had bought to the door before unlocking it. Pushing it open, he saw no lights either downstairs or upstairs and it was totally silent.

He carried the bags to the kitchen, and then climbed the stairs. Through the door, he could see Mya curled up on the bed, the fan gently lifting her hair.

He quietly went back to the kitchen and put everything away. Then rummaging through cupboards, he located a toaster and a pan to make the eggs in. While things were cooking, he washed and sliced the strawberries. He set the small cafe table with silverware, using folded paper towels for napkins.

When the eggs were ready, and the toast buttered, he headed upstairs. Circling the bed, he saw she was asleep again. He squatted down, calling her name.

Her eyes were unfocused when she opened them. "I drank all the water," she responded in a voice like a small child's.

He reached out and slipped his hand under her shoulder. "Then, let's get you some food."

Sitting up, she blinked as she fully came awake and looked at him. "Colton?"

"I told you I would be back and I have supper ready. Maybe artists can live on inspiration and pixie dust, but construction workers need something more substantial."

The pressure of his hand urged her off the bed. "Okay?" he asked as she stood up.

She nodded.

"I'm going to walk with you down the stairs. You feel shaky or lightheaded, you grab on, understand?" He led the way out of the bedroom, and then matched her pace down the stairs; watching closely for any wavering. She was slow, but steady.

Colton was gratified as she ate the dinner and dessert without urging or prompting, although silently. After dinner, she sat quietly as he cleared up and washed the dishes. By the time he had everything cleaned up, her eyes were drooping.

"Let's put you to bed," he said.

"I need to lock the door after you leave."

"I'm not leaving. I'm staying tonight to keep an eye on you."

She looked up and he could read the apprehension in her eyes.

"Mya, if I wanted to take advantage of you, I would have done it this afternoon when you were so far out of things. I promise you are safe." He held out his hand.

*****

Once Colton had her tucked into a bed, he sat on the stairs, staring into the deepening dusk. One part of him was the happiest it had been in maybe his whole life just being here, and knowing Mya was asleep only feet from him. The other part was equally as miserable not knowing how, or, if he could repair his relationship with her. After spinning and playing out dozens of reconciliation scenarios in his head, he yawned widely. He was tired and although the clock was barely leaning on ten, he got up to lock the door and switch off the lights.

Upstairs, he used his toes to push off his athletic shoes before lying down on the bed, carefully keeping much of the queen-size mattress between Mya and himself. She didn't stir.

He looked up through the skylight at the stars. It was almost a full moon and its light was touching the garlands making them seemingly twinkle. He slowly rolled on his side. Mya was on her back, her hand curled beside her face. He fell asleep watching her.

*****

As early morning light flooded the room, Colton felt something like the touch of a butterfly wing on his face. He kept his eyes closed as her finger drifted across his forehead, down the side of his face and along his jaw, ending with a delicate tracing of his lips before withdrawing. He heard the rustle of the sheets as Mya turned over and then felt the bed shift slightly as she got up. Keeping his eyes closed to preserve her privacy, he dozed back off.

Waking abruptly, he grabbed for his cell phone which he had set on the floating shelf by the bed. It said the time was 8:25 a.m. Colton realized his backpack was leaning against the shelving unit when he swung his legs over the edge of the bed. He distinctly remembered leaving it sitting on the floor next to the counter. Fresh towels and washcloths were set out on the old dresser she had converted for storage in the bathroom. Glancing into the kitchen as he came down the stairs, Colton was surprised to see a Keurig coffee maker sitting on the counter, together with a mug and a box of K-cups. He could see Mya sitting on the porch through the open front door. He detoured through the kitchen before heading out into the sun with his freshly brewed coffee.

"How are you feeling?" he asked as he sat down beside her.

She blushed self-consciously. 'I am so sorry to have been a total pain in the ass and messing with your weekend. Thank you, though, for making sure I survived to do stupid another day."

"Mya, you weren't stupid. You just overestimated your ability to deal with the heat. Two of the guys I work with, who are a lot bigger and stronger than you, had to leave early yesterday because it was getting to them."

She studied the contents of her mug for a moment, then forced a smile. "Anyway, I'm feeling fine so you are relieved of any further responsibility. Hopefully, your weekend plans aren't too screwed up."

"My plans are pretty much right here."

Mya stared ahead before setting her cup down and facing him. "Colton, I think you are an amazing person, but I don't do magic well."

His eyebrows pulled together. "Magic?"

"Yes. You know, now you see them, now you don't. It's totally okay if I'm not what interests you, but I can't seem to be as neutral about you. I'm not putting that on you. It's my problem. But I'm just not very good at relationships that are all about drama. If you don't want to be with me, I'm cool with it. But then please just stay away. I don't want to spend any more time looking for someone who's not there."

It was Colton's turn to stare into his coffee. She was both admitting she had feelings for him, but also asking him to stay away because she was assuming he felt nothing for her. He couldn't blame her since he was the one who had vanished for what? Almost seven weeks?

"I don't think I can stay away because you are the only thing I'm interested in, so please don't ask me to."

She shook her head sadly. "I'm sorry, Colton, I just can't do games."

Looking away, he heard Duncan's voice booming in his head. Mya doesn't lie. He wouldn't either.

He sat his cup down and clasped his hands together, leaning his forearms on his thighs. "When we first saw each other, I never learned your last name. One of the girls who works at Deuces told me who you were after seeing us at the Caverns. That's when I found out you had grown up on Rich Ridge... I'm sorry, it's what us poor kids called Quail Crest, and your dad was Jack Parker. I figured you were just a spoiled princess getting her kicks by slumming with a construction guy who worked on her dad's projects. I thought your stories about the renovation, selling your car, and stuff were just to hide who you really were. It pissed me off so I stayed away."

Hearing nothing but silence, he glanced at her. She looked like somebody had slapped her hard.

"If you thought that was me before, what makes you think it isn't me now?" Her voice was small and tight.

"The first day at the center, I saw and heard you with your dad. You could have been a stray mutt for all he seemed to care. Between that and a conversation with Duncan, I realized I had been totally wrong about everything, but then I couldn't figure out how to tell you what a prick I had been."

"So the whole 'save Mya' bit yesterday was just to soothe your conscience?"

Colton swung around to face her. "No!"

She was wearing the same forlorn look he had seen when her dad walked away. It twisted his heart. He gripped her face between his hands. "You have no idea how many times I have driven by here trying to man up enough to come and apologize to you. When I saw you at the center with Wally, it was like someone gut punched me, but you were so quiet and remote I assumed I had blown it completely. What happened yesterday was a friggin' miracle as far as I am concerned because when you desperately needed someone, that someone could be me."

Her eyes were unconvinced.

In response, he lowered his head intending to just brush his lips over hers, but they stayed there as the kiss grew longer and deeper.

He leaned her back until she rested on the porch with his arm under her neck. Although she had braced her hand against his chest at first, it travelled up until it rested on his shoulder.

Finally, he lifted his head. He lightly stroked her cheek. "I've blown so much time with you I don't want to lose any more. Please, can we do a reset?"

"No more vanishing acts?"

"You can implant a tracking device if it will make you feel better."

"I would like to think your word would be enough."

"Then, I promise no more vanishing acts."

A heavily accented voice called to them from the sidewalk. "Mya, sweetheart, get a room!"

Colton quickly righted himself while bringing Mya upright as well. She continued the forward motion as she came to her feet and quickly moved down the stairs to where the old gentleman was leaning on his cane, several limp daisies in his hand.

She stopped as he held them out to her. She took them and then flung her arms around his neck, lightly kissing him on the cheek. They spoke for a moment as the man motioned with his hand in the direction of Colton. She hugged him again before heading back to the gallery while he made his way down the block. She stepped past Colton into the house. In the kitchen, she pulled a cheap vase from the large storage hutch and carefully arranged the flowers in it before setting it on the tiny café table.

Colton had followed, carrying both cups. He dumped his out before resetting the coffee machine to brew a new cup.

"And that was?"

"Mr. Stavros. He lives just down the street. He told me he used to pick a flower for his wife every day. She passed away not long after I bought this place. He sometimes brings me flowers now."

"He looked like he was offering an opinion on me."

"He just asked if you were a good man. I told him I wasn't sure yet, but I was willing to find out."

He crossed to her and lifted her chin. Although he would have liked to have picked up where the last kiss left off, he caught the caution in her eyes and dialed back his ardor. Instead, Colton touched his lips to her forehead. "Thank you."

Chapter 14

The day passed quietly. Mya worked on inking in and coloring the drawings she was preparing to share with the center's board of directors on Monday. Colton took charge of food and drink, bringing her sandwiches, and tea. He explored the extent of physical contact she would allow as they interacted. Although slightly above platonic, she carefully maintained boundaries designed not to lead him to places she obviously was not ready to go; the kiss he had initiated on the porch was apparently not to be repeated.

He was pleased with himself, after finding her phone under the counter downstairs, he had been able to put his cell phone number in it and extract her number for his. He also had surreptitiously been able to take a couple of photos of her.

Finally at four o'clock, he stepped behind her and started to massage her shoulders. She made a contented sound and leaned back against his chest. He bent and kissed the top of her head. "So, would taking a break and going out to get something to eat mess up your work schedule completely?"

She smiled up at him. "That sounds perfect. Where'd you have in mind?"

"Does the Sellah do food?"

"Yes, totchos, and they are amazing."

"Let's go there. You might even be able to get a little payback for my screw-ups with a pool game."

"You're on."

It was early enough the place was still essentially empty. They had just sat down when Jacob came up to the table with a glass in each hand. "Okay, beer slushy and Hefe. Am I right?"

81

Colton looked up at him in amazement. "Dude, I was only in here once weeks ago. How did you remember?"

"That is classified information. You two want anything else?"

"A fully loaded totcho for two?" Mya said as she looked at Colton.

He nodded his agreement, then gestured to the pool table. "Let's get it over."

After selecting their cues, he broke and managed four balls. Mya ran the rest of the table. The second time he got two before Mya ran the table. He was just losing his third game when Jacob called.

"We can interrupt the massacre for food if you want or I can keep it warm if you prefer to continue with the bloodletting."

Colton put his cue back while Mya finished clearing the table and then placed her cue in the rack.

Jacob watched their return. "It's either love or stupidity," he said, shaking his head at Colton.

After spearing a couple of tots with his fork, Colton asked. "Okay, how did you get so good?"

"I played hours and hours of pool growing up. A pool table was the only piece of furniture in the whole main floor of our house, other than a couple of raggedy bar stools in the kitchen we brought from the camp trailer we lived in before moving to up on 'Rich Ridge'."

Colton looked at her. "You lived in a camp trailer?"

Mya popped a tater tot in her mouth. 'Yeah, until I was six. It was parked at my mom's folk's house." Her brow furrowed. "There's a lot I don't really know. Mom died when I was a baby so I never knew her. I vaguely remember my grandparents. I think they took care of me while Dad was getting his business going. Anyway, there was this really awful fight one night. It was Dad, and, I guess, my grandparents. Afterward, Dad tossed everything we had in the back of his pickup and we left. We lived for a while in a motel, and then moved into the house on Quail Crest."

"With only a pool table?"

"Actually, it didn't show up until I was in middle school. I kinda think Dad couldn't afford furniture when we first moved in and by the time he could, he didn't care."

She suddenly had a wicked little smile.

"What?" Colton asked leerily.

"I used to just love watching the faces of the skanks he was always dragging home when they came through the front door and the only thing was a pool table in the front room, all his real estate propaganda, blueprints, and yard signs in the dining area, and the broken down kitchen junk we'd used in the camp trailer. It knocked them on their asses every single time they saw this rich guy living like a penniless bum."

"There goes my whole silver-spoon theory."

"More like a take-out spoon. We ate out, ordered in, or got something requiring only nuking to eat. Truthfully, the only time I got good meals was when Duncan's mom, Cecily, or Nancy's mom, Sharon, fed me. Lucky for me they were always willing to do that."

Her words jostled something Duncan had told him. He reached out and took her hand, turning it over. There was nothing. He then took her other hand. Signs of the old cut were still evident. He ran his finger over the scar, thinking how large a cut it must have on a little girl's hand.

"Colton?" Mya's expression was serious. "There is something you need to know about me before things go any further."

Alarm surged through him.

"My cooking skills are pretty nonexistent."

"Your shopping sucks, too, but I think we'll be able to work out some solutions," he answered trying to match her solemnness. "Tell me. Is that the worst of your sins?"

"Probably not," she said with a sigh.

Chapter 15

"So he didn't come home last night. What's the big deal? Can I please remind you, and I know I am repeating myself, he is almost thirty years old. If he's found someone to cozy up with other than his cat, it's a good thing, Wanda," Babs said.

"It's the artist."

"The gal we saw at the Caverns? I thought he hadn't been anywhere near her since then. And it's been what? A couple of months? And how do you know it is the artist, anyway?"

"Remember how we both thought we knew her from somewhere?"

Babs nodded.

"Turns out she is the one who paints the stuff on the window at Deuces."

Babs searched her memory trying to make the connection. "Okay," she answered.

"So she is there Friday painting the window and she conveniently passes out from the heat just as Colton pulls into the parking so she can get him to take her home and babysit her all weekend. He was even doing her damn grocery shopping."

"I thought you said Colton unexpectedly got off early Friday?"

"So?"

"You're telling me this female was able to know in advance Colton was going to get off early and he was coming to Deuces instead of, say, heading straight home or stopping for a cold beer just so she could topple off a ladder, pretending to be overcome by heat, exactly as Colton is available to catch her. It sounds more like it was an honest to god coincidence."

Wanda looked irritated at the idea as she took a swallow of beer.

"What exactly do you have against the woman anyway?"

"She's not one of us. She was raised up on Quail Crest. Her dad is Jack Parker."

"Damn, girl, what is the problem? Your son is with the daughter of the wealthiest man in town and you want to break it up because she is 'not one of us'. What the hell are we?"

"We're poor, that's what we are. You think a woman like her is going to want to hang around with likes of us? No way. And if Colton hangs with her long enough, she might make him forget where he came from, too."

"So your son might just have a chance to get his golden ticket punched because of her and you would rather he stay on the wrong side of the tracks, sharing a house with you, and his bed with a cat."

"He's shared beds with more than the cat, at least according to some of the girls at the store. I just wish he would pick one of them."

"Why?"

Wanda's voice took on an edge. "Because I know them. I was one of them when I met Johnny. I'm still one of them."

Bully for you, Babs thought, but is that all you really want for your son? She looked over at her friend and realized Wanda was genuinely determined to control Colton's life. Looking away, she wondered just how far Wanda would be really willing to go in heading off any plans Colton might have for himself which didn't align with her plans for him.

*****

After their dinner at the Sellah, Colton reluctantly gathered up his backpack to head home. Mya walked him to the door.

"See you tomorrow?"

"I'm going to be finishing the designs and then going to Nancy and Wally's so he has them for the meeting on Monday."

Disappointment nipped Colton. "I don't know what's going to happen on the job next week. They are really pushing to get our part of the work done by the first of September. Unless the weather breaks super-hot again, the contractor has told us it's gonna mean some long hours so we can get our butts out of there in order to get the finishing guys in."

Oddly, Mya found herself relieved. She needed space to sort out her feelings. She knew she was deeply attracted to Colton, but her feelings were colored by her trust in him being pretty much in the basement. His current words might be nothing more than another opportunity to disappear regardless of anything he had said earlier.

She answered with a neutral smile and a nod of her head. "I understand," was all she said.

In her simple uncomplaining action, Colton glimpsed just how very far he had fallen from any grace he might have once had with her. The chance she was allowing him was by no means guaranteed. In fact, she was still giving him the opportunity to walk away if he wished to; knowing if he did, he could never walk back again.

"If you need anything, call me," he said as he tugged his cell phone from his back pocket. "I put my number in your phone."

"Thank you, again, for your care and concern," she said.

He touched her lips with his before heading to his truck.

She had already disappeared back in the gallery by the time he started the truck. He let it idle for a moment before shifting it into gear and pulling away. She had again unsettled him. He was much more used to women who hung on so tight they left fingerprints on him.

*****

He came through the door at home to discover his mother and Babs apparently engaged in binge watching some series on Netflix. He passed through the front room without comment. Babs noted Wanda did not ask anything either.

It wasn't until he was returning from starting a load of laundry his mother spoke to him. "So what do you want for dinner?" she asked.

"I ate already. Thanks, though."

"I suppose you fed her, too."

Babs caught the yellow spark of danger in Colton's dark brown eyes. He responded by going into his room and closing the door.

She quietly shook her head. One of Wanda's big issues was she rarely caught warning signs until things blew up in her face.

*****

Although beautiful, Cinnamon was not the best subject in front of a camera. Her photos usually looked like somebody famous avoiding the paparazzi. After taking and deleting numerous shots, Colton finally captured the picture he wanted. He sent it to Mya.

Fortunately, she had just lifted the inking pen away from her drawing because she jumped when her phone went off. She looked at it puzzled. There was a text message from Colton. When she opened it, she saw a picture of a snoozing Siamese curled up. It simply said "Sleep Tight. C+C"

She grabbed a piece of paper and quickly sketched the cat identical to the picture. She then added a dream cloud about its head with mice toys, bowls of milk, fish treats, and feathers. She photographed it, and sent it back with the message "Sweet Dreams, C+C".

*****

Wanda was confused by her son's relationship. Although he apparently stopped by most nights, he was always home before ten; on the weekends, by midnight. When he was home, he never spoke of her, and rarely did she hear his phone signal a call or text.

When he finally left his phone where she could check it, she found only a couple of pictures of the person she always referred to in her mind as 'the artist'. One was a profile of her looking down at something while holding a pen in her hand. Another, taken from the back, showed her standing on a porch while her long hair rippled out in the wind. The final one showed her sitting cross-legged on the floor, head turned as she laughed at something. It was evident she was unaware Colton was sneaking pictures of her. As she studied them, Wanda had to admit she was a beautiful woman.

Their few text messages were equally innocuous. No emotional declarations, sexting, saccharine words, or drama as she had seen when she had checked his phone in prior relationships. This was playing out differently and for some reason it made her feel very uneasy.

Chapter 16

As late spring turned into summer, and summer headed towards fall, Colton was scrupulous in being open with Mya; rebuilding her trust in him little by little. Although there were rooms in their past they were not willing to open to each other yet, they were establishing the little routines, in-jokes, and recognitions which were molding them into a couple.

Colton occasionally tested the boundaries, finding a bit more room now and then. He caught glimpses in Mya's eyes she physically desired him as well, but when he pushed in that direction she would immediately pull back; tamp down the fire.

The dog days of latter August arrived, heavy with heat-saturated air. The leaves hung tired and dusty from the trees and people were beginning to eagerly anticipate the crisp days of autumn just a couple of weeks away.

Colton came through the front door of the gallery after work on Friday. Looking up the steps, he saw Mya leaning over her work table. She was wearing a gauzy peasant top over cutoffs. Her long legs and feet were bare.

He peeled off to the kitchen to get a beer before climbing the steps. He took a drink of the cold brew before leaning over to lightly kiss the nape of Mya's neck with his wet lips.

"Mmmm, that feels good," she said as she turned around.

Colton set his beer on the table and pulled her loosely into his arms. 'I think I can do better," he said as he kissed her. As the kiss intensified, he moved his hands down her sides and then slipped them up under her top. It was one of his 'test the boundaries' moves that always elicited his arms being carefully pushed away as their lips separated.

When nothing happened, he pulled her tighter against him, raising his head to look at her. That she wanted him was plain in her expression. He kept one arm around her as he reached under her knees, lifting, and carrying her to the bedroom.

Standing her on her feet, he lifted her top over her head, letting it flutter away in the breeze of the fan. He was amused to note her blue gingham long line bra was more modest than what some of the females were wearing in the streets.

Colton pulled his own tee-shirt off before once again picking her up and laying her in the bed. He lay down beside her, reveling in the feel of her bare skin against his. He kissed her deeply. As his hand slid a bra strap off her shoulder, he felt her begin to tremble. When his fingers glided across her collarbone and down towards her breasts, he realized she was actually shaking.

He raised up on his elbow. "Mya?"

He could see the panic in her face and feel her body going rigid. He touched her cheek. "Mya, are you a virgin?"

"No," she whispered.

He studied her with concern. "Did someone hurt you?"

Shame flooded her face as she turned her head away from him.

"Do you want to stop now? We can."

She turned back to look at him. He could see the war between desire and fear in her eyes.

He held her face in his hand, lightly brushing his thumb over her lips. "Will you trust me?"

She gazed a long moment into his eyes before slipping her arms around his neck and pulling herself up against him. "Yes," she breathed against his mouth.

Slowly and gently he explored her body while guiding her in exploring his. Touching, tasting; hands and mouths brought them to the place where clothing no longer impeded them. The primordial fire etched into blood and bone ignited. When she opened to him, Colton slipped in; moving slowly as their two bodies found mutual rhythm. When Mya drew in her breath and held it while arching under him, his body released in answer.

They lay in their tangle of arms and legs as passion quieted into afterglow. "I didn't know it could be like that," Mya breathed softly.

Drawing her in with his arms, he felt the wall of protection she had kept around herself crumble. She wouldn't need it anymore. He would be her safety.

Colton didn't go home that night.

Chapter 17

Crisp mornings were signaling summer was almost done. Colton began to wear his long sleeved Henleys over his tee-shirts when he left the gallery in the early hours for work. He was spending some of his free time there; consequently the volume of his clothes was growing as he brought changes. Mya cleaned out one of the two dressers in the walk-in closet. She washed, folded, and neatly put his things away. He chided her for it, pointing out he had handled his own laundry since middle school. She countered he was also doing nearly all the cooking when he was there, so this was her contribution. She was careful not to mention his piling things needing to be washed in the corner of the room severely stressed the thread of Obsessive Compulsive Disorder running through her psyche.

Colton was also beginning to notice what her friends already knew. Mya went deeply silent at times when her emotions were overwhelmed or she was vulnerable. He witnessed it firsthand the last week of August. The construction crew was going to meet their deadline to be out of the building by September 1.

Mya had been awarded the contract to paint the graphics throughout the building. She was to begin the project at the same time as the finishers. Then Wally and Nancy called and said they needed to stop by and talk to her about it.

Because of his relationship with Mya, Wally had extended Colton friendship as the two men were in frequent contact during the building renovation. He had met Nancy a few times when she had stopped in to either see Wally or take photos of the progress for a newsletter they apparently sent regularly to donors.

When the couple arrived, they exchanged pleasantries before Wally told Mya they needed to talk. He led the way to the upper floor. Colton looked at Nancy, noting her distress as she watched them ascend.

She caught Colton's eyes on her, and motioned for him to follow her outside. They sat on the porch. "My husband has the unenviable job of sucker punching Mya right now," she said quietly.

Colton pushed up to his feet, turning in the direction of the door.

"There's nothing you can do, Colton. It is one of the ugly facts of nonprofit life the people donating the money sometimes attach irrational stipulations." She motioned for him to sit back down on the porch. "One of the members of the Board of Directors, who is also a huge donor, has convinced the rest of the Board to cancel Mya's contract to do the walls and let his bored, socialite daughter who suddenly fancies herself an artist do them instead."

Colton looked at Nancy in disbelief. "Mya was counting on the work!"

Nancy nodded miserably. "I know. Instead of doing beautiful art, warm and dry inside a building, she will once again be out in the weather painting windows and keeping her frozen fingers crossed the merchants pay her promptly."

"She collapsed painting the window at Deuces when we had that streak of super-hot weather back in May. They had to call the paramedics."

Nancy looked startled, "She didn't tell me—" then she looked resigned as she sighed. "Of course she didn't. Mya never shares anything the rest of us might think is important to know."

Silence stretched between them for some moments before Colton broke it. "Nancy, do you know of anyone who may have hurt Mya when they... er... in a bedroom situation?"

Nancy's face went grim. "Victor." Anger still flashed in her eyes when she glanced at Colton. "Jack used to take on young men he considered promising to intern with him. When Mya was barely 20, he chose a guy who seemed to have it all. He was good-looking, from a respected family, hard-working, and could charm the stripes off a zebra; all of which served to hide the fact he was really a sadistic, manipulative bastard.

"Victor saw Mya when Jack asked him to drop some documents off at the house. She has always been beautiful, in addition to being Jack Parker's daughter, and Victor went after her with every trick he was capable of. Being both young and naïve, Mya was the perfect prey.

"Once the hook was set, his true colors began to show. He was possessive, controlling, and abusive. Because Mya keeps so much to herself, no one knew what was actually happening. Fortunately, Jack walked in one night just in time to see Victor grab Mya, backhand her, and throw her against the wall.

"Jack broke the SOB's arm and dislocated his shoulder. Then he made sure everybody who was anybody knew exactly what Victor had done. He so thoroughly destroyed the guy's reputation he couldn't get a job shoveling roadkill around here. He ended up just disappearing.

"It was the one time Jack actually came through for his daughter. And, no, I don't know any more details than what I've told you. Mya never spoke of it." The door opened behind them. Nancy and Colton stood and turned. Wally looked thoroughly haunted.

Mya's face was composed albeit pale. "You okay?" Nancy asked.

"It is what it is," Mya said with a tremulous smile. And those were the only words Colton ever heard her say about it.

Later as he held her, he could feel the weight of the disappointment in her body. He stroked her face as he looked into her eyes. "It's okay to cry. I don't mind if my shoulder gets wet."

Her smile was stoic. "If they make you cry, they win."

Chapter 18

The next morning, Colton was filling his travel mug with coffee from the Keurig while Mya was sipping tea at the little table; her sketchpad open as she worked on a harvest design for one of her window customers when her cell phone sounded. She answered, putting it on speaker.

"Mya?"

"Hey, Steve, what's going on?"

"We had a little scare last night. Kelly started to have contractions. They got them stopped, but the doctor has ordered her to stay off her feet. My mom is coming to help with the kids but Kelly is stressing about the flea market. She is insisting I handle the booth for her this Saturday. She says if she doesn't show up, she loses her stall space." Panic was now creeping into his voice. "Mya, I don't know anything about the stuff she sells other than it takes up a ton of room in the garage. Kelly will worry the whole day I am absolutely destroying her business, and with good cause! What do I do?"

"How about I show up and help?"

"Oh, god, you'd be a lifesaver. Kelly says you are the only one she trusts."

"Give her my love and tell her to just concentrate on finishing baking the current bun."

"Six more weeks. Hey, where did you get that? Give it to me now. Come back here." The call disconnected.

Colton bent to kiss her goodbye. "I need to go home tonight. Cinnamon is getting stressed and not eating again according to Mom. Also she and Babs need a few things done to get their places ready for winter."

She smiled at him. "Cinnamon may have tumbled to the fact you are cheating on her. It may take a diamond kitty collar to earn her forgiveness this time."

"Hopefully, I can get by with a can of very expensive albacore tuna. I'll see you tomorrow after work."

Mya waited until she had heard his engine start and the truck pull away from in front of the gallery before she let her shoulders slump. Cinnamon wasn't the only one who got a little stressed when he left. But pity parties would have to wait. She had income to replace so she better be about putting her nose to the proverbial grindstone.

She picked up her sketchpad and headed upstairs. It was time to check the inventory in her Etsy shop and get some fresh pictures up on her website to lure in new commissions.

The day disappeared as she focused on various aspects of her business. Mya drew up her quarterly detailed income projections. She was coming into the season where she needed to make as much money as possible to tide her over the first quarter of the coming year when business was slow to nonexistent.

She had a slight headache by the time she was done. After heading downstairs, she realized her phone was still on the table. She opened it looking to see if she had missed a message from Colton. The absence of any message initiated a little hope he might decide to come back tonight anyway. She fixed a cup of tea and went out on the porch to breathe in the evening air.

He didn't come back that night or the next night either. He sent a brief message saying there was more to do than he had expected and it was going to take longer. He would see her when he was done. Mya hated the fact she was back watching for him when day two melted into day three of his absence.

*****

She tried to keep her mind from focusing on missing him. Duncan dropped off some bags of bark dust for her. She mowed her lawn, then weeded, cleaned and mulched in the front flower beds for winter. She repainted the treads on the steps and replaced the spent petunias in the planters sitting on either side of the stairs with mums.

She restocked her window paints with yellows, oranges, browns, and dark reds for the seasonal windows she was scheduled to paint.

She updated her window design portfolio and spent a day cold calling for additional business. In between, she was creating new items for her e-store, working late into the night to avoid crawling into an empty bed.

By Saturday morning, not having heard anything more from him all week, she assumed he wasn't coming back. She put the Keurig away before catching the bus to the flea market. She would bag his clothes when she got home and figure out how to get them to him.

Chapter 19

*T*he relief on Steve's face when she walked up to the stall was comical. They spent a busy hour and a half getting everything set up; finishing with time to spare before the market officially opened.

"So where's Colton this morning? Sleeping in?"

Mya shrug was noncommittal. "I'm not sure. He's been at his mom's since Monday helping her and her friend get their places ready for winter. I haven't really heard from him this week."

Steve looked at her closely. He saw the all too familiar neutral expression. "Seems a bit odd for a man who's in love."

"He never said that."

"He's never told you he loves you?"

She shook her head.

"So what is it? You're just a friend with benefits?"

"Maybe. Once… " she said softly.

The first customers arrived at the stall. Steve stepped back as Mya engaged them. He was confused by her words. He would have sworn Colton was crazy in love with her. He had seen the man's face when he looked at Mya, but she was saying the guy went home to his mother and hadn't bothered to contact her for a week. Colton was either a first-rate actor or an absolute idiot.

The day became farcical when the number of males stopping by to hit on Mya almost exceeded the number of customers interested in the goods. They ended up divvying duties. Mya sold and Steve deflected the men.

By three o'clock, Steve could see Mya was drooping. She hadn't had time to eat anything all day and had barely touched the tea he had brought her. Though the corridors between the booths were virtually empty of people, the vendors couldn't officially tear down until five. He sent her over to say hi to Emma, knowing Emma would make her eat something and rest.

Steve was both surprised when Colton walked up to the booth, and irritated.

"Hi, Steve. I thought Mya was going to be helping you today?"

"She's been busting her butt all day. I just made her go take a break."

"So how did it go?"

"We would have made a fortune if all the guys who flocked here hitting on her had actually bought something. Although, one did offer to buy everything we had if she was included in the deal."

"You watched out for her," Colton said sharply.

"You bet. Although, I would have thought that should have been your job."

"I've been stuck at my mom's place getting a bunch of stuff done so the house was ready for winter. Mya knew. I texted her."

"According to her, you sent her one text in what? Six days? That's definitely the key to making a woman feel like she matters to you."

"Mya knows she matters to me."

"Actually, she doesn't. She thinks she might have been a friend with benefits for a while, now she doubts even that."

"Come on, man, I love her!"

"Have you ever told her?"

"Of course, I..." Colton stopped. "I guess I have thought it a million times, but I don't think I have actually said the words out loud to her."

"Why not?"

"I don't know. Maybe I assumed she would know how I felt."

"Colton, why are you with Mya? Just so you have a beautiful woman for arm candy and to have sex with? You say you're in love with her, but do you have any plans that might include something more long range, maybe even permanent?"

"You mean like a ring? Are you telling me Mya is expecting a ring?"

"Absolutely not."

"Then what is she expecting from me?"

"To be dumped."

Colton stared at Steve. The man was completely serious.

"She told you that?"

"Mya never shares things hurting her. It is one of the most irritating things about her. The only way you know something is tearing her apart is she shows absolutely no emotion. Then you wait to see what she never mentions again to figure out what it was."

Colton flashed back to the evening Wally told her about losing the contract. No one would have guessed she had taken a severe hit from her expression when she came out on the porch. She had also never said another word about it.

"Mya deserves to be the priority in someone's life; not just a convenience to be set aside and ignored when something else comes up. I'm pretty sure she's convinced you aren't coming back any time soon, if at all. Maybe now would be a good time for you to move on since you obviously aren't committed to a relationship with her."

"I'm committed," Colton snapped back.

"So committed you don't even check in with her for a week to see if she is okay? So committed you forget to mention you supposedly love her? So committed she feels she was nothing more than just a passing fling that has burned out? I'd say your idea of what constitutes a commitment needs work— big time. There is a whole helleva lot more to a relationship than the bed."

"I know."

"Then prove it or let go so maybe she can find someone who will make her feel loved as she should be."

His words sliced through Colton. "Don't tell her I was here," Colton said, turning and heading toward the street.

Steve watched as he cut between two booths and disappeared. "I'd hoped you were a better man," Steve said *sotto voce*. He desperately hated Mya was being shit on again.

Chapter 20

Colton drove to the gallery because he knew Mya wouldn't be back for a while. Getting out of his truck, he noticed the work she had done prepping for the coming winter. He sat on the porch stairs letting Steve's words wash through him.

What the hell kind of man does just walk out the door, leaving a woman he claims to be in a relationship with alone for days without even sending her a text? He texted his mother every day he spent at the gallery to check on his cat, and when his mother said Cin needed him, he trotted right home to sleep with a cat; leaving Mya to sleep alone.

A realization began to form in his mind. He pretty much bent to his mother's demands and complaints without thought or question. He knew she was totally against the idea of Mya in his life. She was openly derogatory about her, never using her name, just calling her 'the artist', and scathing of the time he spent with Mya. He also knew his mother got into his phone whenever he was careless enough to leave it around. In a weird way, he had made himself believe he was somehow protecting Mya if he didn't actually communicate with her so his mother had nothing to use against her.

The same thing with telling her he loved her. If he kept it to himself, then it remained a secret his mother couldn't discover.

He came to his feet when he recognized he had been basing his whole relationship with Mya on keeping his mother happy. He began to pace up and down the walkway wondering how and when he ended up some kind of puppet to be yanked around by his mom's whims and wants exclusively.

Did it start after his dad committed suicide or before? He couldn't exactly remember when the litany of "you won't leave me alone like your dad"; "you're gonna take care of your momma, aren't you"; "good boys want their mommas to be happy" started. Somewhere between then and now, she had manipulated him into believing his sole function was being responsible for what she wanted. If what he wanted didn't meet her approval, then he wasn't allowed to want it.

He stopped and stared at the gallery. What he wanted more than anything was here. It was time to emancipate himself. Colton headed to his truck.

Once at the house, he went to the kitchen to get some garbage bags for his clothes and Cinnamon's cat carrier. Swinging it around the end of the counter, he knocked a stack of papers and mail on the floor. Groaning, he bent to pick them up. One was his mother's pay stub. He was startled when he saw how much she was bringing home as a manager at Deuces. He had been turning over half of his earnings to her since he was sixteen years old so she would be able to make the mortgage. According to the slip in his hand, she earned ample to pay the mortgage; something she had failed to tell him. Instead, she perpetuated the mortgage lie apparently to keep him trapped in her web.

Colton tossed everything on the counter and went to begin shoveling his clothes into the bags. He moved on to disconnecting his TV and game system; cushioning the components between bags of clothes in the truck bed. He finished loading Cinnamon's litter box, litter, and food on the floor board in the cab. Everything else he owned was in the truck bed. He had only to load up Cinnamon and he was out of here.

He swung the truck door closed and headed back, working the house key off his key ring when his mother's car pulled into the drive. She and Babs got out. Wanda walked over and looked in the bed.

"What the hell are you doing?" she asked as she followed him into the house.

"Something I should have done a decade ago. I'm getting out of here."

"You can't. You know I'll lose the house."

Crossing to the counter, he picked up her pay stub and waved it in front of her face. "Bullshit. Besides now you can rent out my room."

"Who's going to take care of me if you don't? I'm your mother. You owe me that."

"You aren't ready for a nursing home yet, so you can take care of yourself," he countered. "I've already paid with the first thirty years of my life. You'll just have to put the rest on my tab."

"You're just like your father. A self-centered, worthless piece of shit."

Colton stared at her. "Is that what you told dad? Is that why he ended up using this?" Opening a cupboard he reached high into a back corner and pulled out a revolver. "Did he kill himself to make you happy?"

"Too bad you aren't man enough to do the same."

He shoved it under his jaw, not noticing the broken front sight gouged a furrow in his skin. Blood began to trickle down his neck as he held it there.

"So spattering blood and brains all over the kitchen is proof of love. What then? You put me in a jar on your dresser along with Dad and we still all hang out; one happy family?"

The acrimony in her eyes was clear as she watched him. "You haven't got the balls."

Colton pulled the trigger.

Chapter 21

He lowered the gun after it dry-fired. "Now I'm dead to you," he said quietly. He dropped it on the counter and shoved by to pick up Cinnamon's carrier.

Wanda looked into Babs' horrified eyes. "He knew the gun was empty."

Babs stared back at her. "But did you?"

Colton started the truck and sat idling long enough to block his mother's phone number. Then he left without looking back. It was over here. Everything he wanted lay ahead.

The minute he pulled in front of the gallery, he felt unsure. He had operated on the presumption Mya would welcome him back. Steve's words cast shade over that. Had he messed things up so badly he and Cinnamon would have to live in a motel somewhere? Regardless, he was determined to say the words he should have said months ago. If it was too late to make a difference, at least she would know she wasn't just a 'convenience'.

Looking closely, he saw the lights were on. He got out of the truck, reaching back in the cab to lift the cat carrier out. At the door, he hesitated about just walking in and, instead, knocked. He could see Mya coming out of the kitchen with a puzzled look on her face. He watched her reaction to seeing him. She looked both startled and cautious.

"Colton?" she said opening the door. Her eyes were immediately drawn to the trail of blood running from under his jaw to his tee-shirt. She reached up, urging him to raise his chin so she could see before grabbing his wrist. "What happened?"

He set the carrier on the counter as Mya pulled him toward the kitchen, pushing him into one of the café chairs. Grasping his chin, she carefully tilted his head so she could examine the wound closely.

"Stay put," she said as she went to the back wall hutch and pulled out her medical bin. She cleaned, salved and bandaged the gash.

"How did it happen?" she asked as she helped Colton get his bloodied tee-shirt off.

"There must have been a rough place on the gun barrel when I jammed it against my neck."

Mya took Colton's face in her hands, bending so she looked him directly in the eyes. "Why were you pointing a gun there?" she asked in a frightened voice. "Were you trying to kill yourself?"

He leaned his forehead against hers. "No. I was having a fight with my mother about finally moving out and things got out of control."

"You must have scared her to death."

"Not exactly. She pretty much told me to pull the trigger," he said as he leaned back against the wall.

Mya studied him as she washed the dried blood off his neck and chest. He was drawn and ashy; the usual glow in his brown eyes muddied. She tugged at his arm, urging him to his feet. "Come with me," she said as she guided him out of the kitchen and towards the stairs.

In the bedroom, she knelt down and dragged his shoes off before firmly pushing him flat on the bed. She drew the throw blanket up over his bare shoulders, then leaned in and very lightly kissed his jaw above the bandage. "Sleep," she whispered.

*****

Downstairs, she noticed the carrier and looked inside. A Siamese cat was huddled in the back.

"Cinnamon?" she asked. The cat responded with a soft yowl.

Looking out the window, she saw plastic garbage bags and a TV in the back of Colton's truck. She looked back at the cat. "Well, those can't stay there. Will you be okay while I get his stuff in here?" Cinnamon yowled again.

Mya was surprised at how little stuff Colton actually had; clothes, TV, gaming system and games, and a small box of personal papers. She discovered the litter box, litter, and food when she was locking the doors on the cab.

Once everything was safely stacked along the wall, Mya went into the kitchen and hunted through her mismatched flea market dishes for three bowls. She pulled an oversized placemat out of the storage cabinet and set up a feeding station for Cinnamon.

She pondered the litter box situation. She definitely didn't want it in the kitchen and the exhibit areas were out of the question. Upstairs, she looked around until she found what she felt would be a workable location. Digging out an old failed weaving project to put under it, she added the litter. Time to give Cinnamon the grand tour.

*****

The sound of a voice penetrated Colton's sleep. He slowly opened his eyes and rolled over. The skylight was black with no stars indicating clouds had rolled in. He listened. Mya was talking to someone. He sat up and leaned forward so he could see out the bedroom door. He saw her sitting on the floor next to the work table holding his cat. Cinnamon was being quite attentive, occasionally adding her own yowls to the conversation. He lay back down and listened.

"Now you know where to find your things for however long you are here." She paused. "You are beautiful, Cinnamon. I can see why he was always eager to go home to you. I do apologize for the nights he didn't. It is no fun to share the bed with acres of emptiness. Sometimes when he wasn't here, I'd get a little scared because I know one of these days he is going to go out the door and never come back. When that day comes, you must make sure the next person takes very good care of him. Promise?"

Cinnamon voiced her promise.

Colton stared at the black hole of the skylight. Steve was totally telling him the truth. Mya didn't think she mattered to him. She really believed he was simply passing through her life on the way to something else.

Mya became a silhouette in the doorway as she tiptoed into the bedroom. Colton closed his eyes. Coming around the bed, she carefully set Cinnamon down beside him. She lightly brushed her fingers over his thick shock of hair before leaving. Cinnamon started her raspy purr as she maneuvered herself onto his shoulder.

Colton could hear Mya rummaging in her workspace for a few minutes, then it was quiet. He assumed she had gone downstairs. He stroked Cinnamon. Oddly, his high-strung Siamese cat seemed quite content as she stretched out on the plush throw blanket over his shoulder. Rain began to tap on the skylight. He upended Cinnamon as he sat up abruptly. His stuff was still in the truck bed.

He pulled his shoes back on and dug a Henley out of the drawer in the closet. He finished pulling it down over his chest as he trotted downstairs. Mya was sitting on the floor stitching something out of turquoise blue paisley scraps.

She saw him looking over the bannister. "I was worried everything was going to get rained on or possibly stolen, so I brought it in. Was that alright?"

"More than alright. Thank you."

She set aside what she was working on. Getting up and crossing to him, she tilted his chin to check the bandage before examining his face. "You look like you feel better."

He reached out and took hold of her upper arms. "Mya, there is something I need to tell you." He held on when she went rigid and tried to step back. "As screwed up as I managed to make everything..." His voice softened. "I want you to know I love you, and I'm pretty sure I have since the first time I saw you chasing after that ball of green yarn back in March."

Her eyes were unsure. "You love me?"

He pulled her into a hug which threatened to crush her. "God, baby, I love you so much I can't breathe sometimes while other times my heart feels like it is going to pound right out of my chest."

Mya fought her way out of his arms; pushing him away as she turned toward the window. He could see her face reflected in the darkened glass. Confusion chased by mistrust and then fear swept across her features before her face settled into her look clearly telling him how vulnerable she was feeling. The rapid rise and fall of her shoulders revealed the strength of the emotions tumbling through her.

Following, Colton reached around to take her elbows, turning her to face him. Leaning against the counter, he maneuvered her in between his legs.

"I get it. I have been pretty much blown everything I've ever said to you. Why would you believe anything I say now?" He paused. "Maybe, for all I know, it's the last thing you ever wanted to hear from me."

Her voice was barely audible. "I'm scared. If I let myself believe you really love me, I will be giving you enough room inside my heart to destroy me when you change your mind."

He took her face in his hands, staring straight into her eyes. "Will you trust me?"

They held each other's gaze for long moments, then Mya collapsed against him. "Yes," she whispered. He wrapped his arms around her pulling her in tight against his body. When Mya realized her pelvis was leaning against his crotch, she gave a little wiggle.

In moments, Cinnamon found herself displaced from the bed.

The rain of the night had passed and a rectangle of brilliant blue Indian summer sky was framed in the skylight. Colton felt Mya's body curled against his own. He turned on his side and wrapped an arm over her waist. His hand ended up resting on Cinnamon's blonde fur as she slept tucked against Mya's stomach. At that moment, the world was absolutely perfect.

He pushed up to slip out of bed. Coming around to the other side, he watched as two pairs of almost identical blue eyes sleepily opened up to look at him. He leaned across the bed to kiss both females.

"One of you ladies will be taken to breakfast if you can get your sexy little butt out of bed."

Chapter 22

Cinnamon disappeared while Mya and Colton showered and dressed. Mya was making the bed when Colton headed downstairs. She heard his voice saying "Oh, oh, Cin. Did you have permission to get into those?"

Following him, Mya saw Cinnamon had helped herself to the pink feathers she had been intending to attach to a toy she was making for the cat. She was happily racing and sliding around the wood floor as she chased them.

"She's good. They were going to be for her anyway."

Colton reached out to catch Mya in his arms. "Thank you for being the most amazing person I have ever met. And I am absolutely starved. Let's roll."

Colton wheeled his truck into the parking lot of a chain restaurant. He was just parking when he looked up and said, "Uh-huh. We're outta here. I see my mom's car."

He backed up and headed to the exit. "Any suggestions?" he asked.

"How about Papa's over on Boyle? It's a total dump, but the food is great!"

Mya was right, the place was definitely a dive, however, the plates he saw being delivered when they went in looked delicious.

After ordering, Colton fidgeted with his coffee cup, turning it in circles as Mya watched him.

Finally, he looked up at her. "Baby, I want to ask you to do something. I want you to give up doing the windows at Deuce's."

"Why?"

"My mom manages it, and she is not a very nice person. I learned

115

just how 'not nice' yesterday."

Mya slipped her hand across the table and under his fingers, curling hers into his, just watching him.

Colton looked out the grubby window. "My dad committed suicide when I was thirteen. My mom always claimed it was because he was a worthless wuss. What's sad is I barely knew my dad. Looking back, I can see my mom was always between us; pushing us apart."

He closed his eyes briefly. "I can still hear the gunshot. He was in the garage. She had been in the garage, too. She told me she was trying to talk him out of it, but couldn't."

He went silent. Mya ran her thumb back and forth over his fingers as she waited. He suddenly drew in a huge breath, looking directly at Mya. "I think she pushed him into pulling the trigger."

"The gun yesterday— was it the same— ?"

Colton nodded. "One of the police brought it in the house. He unloaded it and took all the bullets. I didn't want Mom to see it so I got a chair and put it in the highest place I could. She didn't know it was there.

"When we got into the fight yesterday about me leaving, she brought up dad; saying I was a worthless and self-centered POS just like he was. That's when I got the gun down."

"And she really told you to pull the trigger?"

"Pretty much she challenged me to, yes."

Mya's grip tightened on his hand as she reached out to touch the wound on his neck. "Colton, she couldn't have known the gun was unloaded."

Colton stared back.

Their breakfasts were delivered, but even as Colton tucked into his food, Mya could see a gulf of pain behind his eyes.

What kind of person would try to bully their own son into killing himself?

Chapter 23

Although she had warned him it was her busiest time of the year while they settled into their new living arrangements, Colton was surprised how many hours she worked each day. She was usually up and showered before his cell phone alarm went off at 6:30, and it was not uncommon for her to slip back out of bed after she thought he was asleep.

Her prospecting for business windows to paint had added several more to her already burgeoning seasonal calendar. As she relied on the bus to get her around, the projects often involved extra hours. He gently tried to get her to ease up, but she would just silence him with a kiss, assuring him once the new year arrived she would become the proverbial slug as she moved into her slow time.

Colton gradually became accustomed to seeing her periodically 'disappear', as she had months ago at Cactus Flats, which generally played out as it had the first time he saw it. A quick sketch on the nearest piece of blank paper, and then she was back.

Since her art had always been a part of their relationship, Colton adapted to the vagaries of its influence over the woman he loved. He regarded it as having a similar relationship with Mya as he had with Cinnamon; something needing regular affection and attention, but still subservient.

Then he learned it could also be a rival lover with the ability to capture her fully in its thrall. It was one of the rare days when he had been able to keep Mya beside him until he got up. Since he needed the bathroom in order to get ready for work, she had opted to head downstairs wearing her sleep shorts and one of his old Henleys; her

117

long braid frowsy.

By the time he came into the kitchen, she had his travel cup filled with hot coffee and was sitting at the table with her tea. She crumpled a piece of paper and tossed it on the floor for Cinnamon.

As she watched the cat leap, spin, and stalk the paper, her lips parted slightly while her eyes began to study something visible only to her. She didn't even react when Colton bent over and kissed her good-bye. As he stepped away from her, she sprang to her feet, racing up the stairs to her work table. He shook his head with a trace of annoyance and headed out the door.

He was stunned when he came back through it in the evening to discover Mya bent over her work table still in her bed clothes. When she raised her head, she was wearing what looked like a postcoital glow; eyes soft, lips moist, and her face faintly flushed.

He veered directly into the bedroom. It was exactly as it had been when he walked out this morning. Still he felt uneasy. Mya was behaving so far out of character, he wasn't sure which of the flailing emotions coursing through him he should grab and run with. The uncertainty kept him from saying anything to her. He decided to head directly to the shower.

He pulled his Henley and tee-shirt over his head, dropping them on the floor before sitting on the edge of the bed to tug off his shoes and socks. Standing, he began to unbutton his jeans when Mya breathed his name.

Turning his head, he realized she was only inches from him. There was hunger in her eyes while sexual yearning flared off her skin. He reached out, grabbing the back of her head as he brought his mouth down hard on hers. Something in her met his force bringing fierceness to their lovemaking. It drove them longer and deeper until ultimately release came in waves breaking over them repeatedly before they lay emptied against each other.

Mya turned, resting her back against him. Reaching over her shoulder, she gently ran the back of her hand over him. He caught it, holding it in his own until she unconsciously pulled away from him as she rolled onto her side and drifted into sleep.

Colton watched her before slipping out of bed and heading to take his shower. She slept still when he came out of the bathroom and went into the closet to grab clean clothes.

Downstairs, he made himself a fresh cup of coffee. He took her purloined phone to the front porch where he searched through her contacts to locate Nancy's number, sipping as he waited for her to connect.

"Hey, Mya, what's happening, babe?"

"Hi, Nancy. It's actually me."

"Colton? Is something wrong with Mya?"

"I'm not sure. She's really different today."

"Explain."

Colton detailed his observations.

His concerns were met with a chuckle. "Ah, I wondered when you might meet Mya in Ecstasy."

"Ecstasy, like drugs?"

"No, no… like altered state. Mya has never touched drugs. It's when she gets so caught up in an interior vision the rest of the world just doesn't exist until she brings to fruition whatever she sees within her. It's happened since she was a kid. When she was in middle and high school, she would sometimes work literally around the clock until her body simply shut down forcing her into sleep."

"Today, she had this glow about her, like she had been making love with someone while I was at work."

"In a way she had, but it was with the muse driving her creations. Colton, you have to understand Mya doesn't just do art. In her deepest soul, Mya is art. And, like today, she will challenge your perceptions, unsettle you, and behave in ways far removed from the mundane life most people wander through. I'd be willing to bet she's not like anyone else you have ever been with. She doesn't operate the way most women operate."

"No, she doesn't which is why sometimes I don't exactly know what to do with and about her."

"Just keep on doing what you have been so far. Sharing her days; ensuring she eats and rests; and, hopefully, making frequent passionate love to her. Just don't make it a competition between you and her art. That is going to be difficult since you will face a lot of times when it will feel like she is putting it ahead of you. If you do force a competition, you might win because of how much she cares about you, but it will be a hollow victory since it will definitely damage her. Please be careful."

He agreed and then, at Nancy's request, checked Mya's calendar to confirm she had the special preview of the youth center in her schedule. Nancy made him promise he would contact her any time he had concerns before concluding the call.

Disconnecting, he placed the phone on the little table in the kitchen. He may have an understanding now about what had occurred, but he was still unsettled. Regardless of the fact Mya had spent the day with what Nancy called her 'muse,' he was still dogged by a sense she had somehow cheated on him. Colton could hear the shower running upstairs.

He climbed the stairs to her work table. It was littered with elegantly rendered drawings of stylized Siamese cats that looked exactly like Cinnamon; each featured the neutral colored cat engaging with a brilliantly colored and detailed toy like a mouse or a wand of feathers. Even to his untrained eye, they were definitely what would be described as 'works of art'.

Mya came out of the bedroom wearing a towel while blotting her long hair with another. She looked at Colton with a warm smile which gradually faded as he stared back expressionless. His eyes were cold as he held up one of the drawings. "Exploiting my cat for commercial purposes, huh."

"Oh," was all she said before retreating back to the bedroom.

Colton picked up the several half-drunk cups of tea and carried them down to the kitchen.

Mya sat for a long time on the edge of the bed after combing out her hair. She didn't understand why, but it was clear the sight of her was provoking irritation, even hostility, in Colton today. Even his lovemaking bore the edge of anger. She had made some dreadful mistake and she didn't know what it was.

She buried her face in her hands. She grasped she had obviously been living in some kind of romantic fool's world. She thought being loved by someone was a place where you felt safe and wanted, but it didn't seem to work that way for her. She definitely hadn't been safe with Victor and now, apparently, she wasn't going to be with Colton, either.

There was only one thing she could think of to rectify what might be one her 'sins' of today although she wasn't sure it would make anything right between her and Colton. Still it might show him, she hadn't intended to do harm. She forced herself to walk to her work table and began gathering up the artwork.

Mya was struggling to get her breath when she finished. She reached for her bomber jacket. Pulling her slouch beanie out of the pocket, she caught her hair in it. In the closet, she dragged a scarf off the rack to wind around her neck before picking her house key up and shoving it into her pocket.

She silently made her way downstairs. She could hear Colton in the kitchen. She swiftly crossed to the door, opening and closing it carefully behind her. Hiding in the shadows, she cut across the yard to the sidewalk; running until she was sure she couldn't be seen anymore.

She had desperately hoped she would not have to fight this battle again. Why couldn't she just be who she was? Why was she never good enough? If Colton didn't want her as she was, who did he want her to be instead?

And why didn't he see art wasn't just her passion, it was her livelihood. She had to be able to meet the monthly mortgage as well as all the other household expenses. She didn't expect him to contribute even though they were sharing the space. She had been raised to believe it was all on her to keep a roof over her head, regardless of who else might be under it.

She had been so excited about her visions of the cats at play. The images she created felt like something which would have sold well for a long time as prints. She worked so hard trying to reach the point where she could get a break allowing her to have a little breathing room. But it seemed just when something was coming into view, like the contract for the youth center, it sank before it actually reached her. Maybe she wasn't ever going to get there. Maybe all she was destined for was to be the loser finger painter her father thought she was. Still, it didn't matter what the final outcome would ultimately be, she was going to keep giving her work everything she had unless—

Unless she had to choose between her art and Colton.

Chapter 24

It had been quiet for over an hour. Colton headed upstairs. He glanced in the bedroom, noting all his clothes were picked up and, by the different color sheets, the bed freshly changed. All the art that had been on the work table was gone. The mason jars carefully aligned along the side of the bare surface. He circled the wall separating the stairwell from the rest of the room. The area was dark.

He swung back and went into the bedroom. All the spaces were empty. Coming back out, he saw her bomber jacket was missing. Somehow she had managed to leave without him noticing it. He pulled his cell phone out and tapped through to her number. In a moment, he heard her phone ringing on the table in the kitchen; right where he had left it.

Colton headed back down the stairs and out the front the door. A fall fog had settled in. He could barely see to the sidewalk. He felt a surge of panic rising in him. His first impulse was to jump in his truck and start driving around looking for her. He recognized the foolishness of the idea. He could drive all night and never find Mya; especially if she didn't want to be found. All he could really do was wait and hope she made it back safely on her own.

The minutes crawled by over the next hour. His fears were rising to a level approaching unbearable. He paced from the kitchen to the gallery room and back, watching from one window to the next. Occasionally he would climb the stairs even though he knew there was no possible way for her to get past him again.

He had just pulled a beer out of the refrigerator when he heard a crash on the second floor. He raced up the stairs to see Cinnamon had knocked over the wastebasket by the work table and was busily

123

dragging stuff out of it.

"Cin, I am so not in the mood for you," he snapped as he got down on one knee to pick up the debris. Gathering up the paper scraps, a couple floated back out of his hand. Reaching for them again, he stopped. One of them had part of a cat head on it; the other a bit of feathers. He shuffled the pieces he held from hand to hand, identifying bits and pieces of the art he had seen this afternoon on the work table. She had destroyed her beautiful work.

"I didn't mean to do wrong," she said very softly. Colton's head jerked up. Mya stood there looking absolutely gutted as she stared at the shards of her creations in his hand. She turned away and unzipped her moisture-slicked jacket.

Hastily dropping the scraps back in the wastebasket, he crossed the couple of steps to her. He reached out to pull off her damp beanie. She flinched away, stepping back from him.

"Mya! I'm not going to hit you."

She didn't answer, just backed up another step before turning to disappear into the bedroom closet. In a moment, she slipped back out and headed downstairs to the kitchen. He stared after her before following slowly.

She put a cup of water into the microwave to heat before going to open the refrigerator. She stared disinterestedly into it before letting the door swing shut while she went to retrieve her cup. She sat down at the table, slowly dragging a tea bag back and forth in the hot water.

Colton crossed to the counter to fix her a bagel with fruit-infused cream cheese. He brought it to the table, setting it beside her hand. She didn't seem to notice until he carefully took the tea bag away from her and out of the cup.

"Please eat, baby. I'm pretty sure you haven't today." He picked a bagel half up and put it in her hand. She looked at it blankly. He urged her hand toward her mouth. She bit into it. Although she never actually looked at him, he was still able to get her to eat the rest of the bagel. She finished her tea before going upstairs, uncharacteristically leaving her dishes on the table.

Colton cleaned up the kitchen; then shut down the downstairs. When he got to the bedroom, he found she was already asleep in bed so close to the edge, her hair brushed the floor. He set the alarm on his cell phone before crawling in on the opposite side. He understood her comment about 'acres of emptiness' as he looked across to her.

Cinnamon jumped on the bed. He held his hand out to her. She sniffed it disdainfully before stretching herself along Mya's back like some small, self-appointed body guard.

He rolled on his back and stared at the dark skylight. He had done exactly what Nancy had warned him against. Seeking payback for what he perceived was an indiscretion on her part, he had inserted himself between her and her art; wanting a choice—a choice which shattered something in her.

*****

The next morning, Mya was unsurprisingly already up when his alarm went off. Colton assumed she was down in the kitchen as he dressed for work. He grabbed his jean jacket off the coat tree as he passed, noting her bomber jacket was still hanging on it, then he heard the front door close. He sped down the stairs. Looking out the gallery room window, he could see her heading in the direction of the bus stop dressed in her old second hand barn coat with her window painting tote over her shoulder.

Although she usually left a charming little illustration under his travel mug on the days she left before him, today there was nothing. He fixed his coffee and checked Cinnamon's dishes. They were already filled.

He had just gotten into his truck when the bus pulled in down the block and he watched Mya get on. As he started his engine, letting it idle to warm up, it occurred to him he had absolutely no idea where she was going. Although he saw her work scattered around town on various windows, he had no clue when she did what storefront.

Pulling away from the curb, he was unaware he, in fact, believed he was on his way to a real job while Mya was off to some kind of kindergarten play date.

Chapter 25

The construction crew's current project was renovating a former hardware store into a series of professional offices; another Parker project. They had just completed the demolition and were beginning to frame in the different spaces.

Heading out for lunch, the men stopped in the back doorway leading to the parking area. Torrential rains were pouring; a prelude to the approaching winter. They debated whether to wait a few minutes to see if it would lighten up or brave a dash to their vehicles. Colton decided to hang back. He was just going to hit the little convenience store three blocks over for a couple of fried burritos and a drink.

After five minutes, though, the rain was not showing any signs of slowing down. He raced to his truck, glad he hadn't bothered to lock it. By the time he returned, the skies had lightened dramatically and the rain had subsided.

Gary, the crew foreman, pulled in beside him as he got out of his truck. Colton waited for the older man to catch up. "Went to Cuthbert's Deli," Gary held out a bag, as the two walked back to the building. "And, damn, if the young woman who does the window painting around town wasn't working on their window in the middle of the monsoon we just had. There's a little cover there but not enough to protect from the rain blowing in. She had to be soaked to the skin, water was just a streaming off of her, but she put on the sweetest smile when I stopped to ask her if she wasn't about to drown. She said she hoped not because she owed another business a window. Shame the pretty little thing doesn't have anyone who cares

127

about her."

Startled, Colton looked at him. "What makes you think that?"

Gary shrugged. "If she did, they might make sure she had some proper clothes for working out in our Oregon weather instead of an old coat with no waterproofing left in it and raggedy tennis shoes."

They entered the building, making their way to a space piled with lumber which they appropriated as seating. They were followed by a couple of the other crew.

"Hey, Gary, you see the gal painting the window at Cuthbert's? She was something."

"Yeah, I sure wouldn't mind taking her home and drying her off real good," said the other.

All three men watched with surprise as Colton stormed out of the space.

*****

Their comments vexed Colton all afternoon. It bugged him men assumed Mya had no one in her life; therefore was available for whatever dirty thought they chose to throw at her. How much scrambling had she had to do through the years to keep herself out of harm's way?

He thought about last night when Mya had walked for two hours in the fog without even her phone. Had she felt safer alone in the night than she did with him after he had been a first class ass to her? Did Mya believe she was still as alone as the men this afternoon seemed to think she was?

*****

The rain was falling again when he pulled up in front of the gallery. Colton dashed from the truck to the porch. Lying outside the door was the coat Mya had worn. When he picked it up, he discovered it was so soaked by the rain it was heavy. Underneath were her equally soaked tennis shoes and mismatched socks.

Inside, he found the kitchen littered in paint jars, brushes, spray bottles, and rags with the emptied tote drying on a towel. Her sopped jeans and sweatshirt were in the sink.

Upstairs, she was in the bed, curled in a tight ball under the blankets; her hair wrapped in a towel.

"Mya?"

She opened her eyes. "I got cold," she whispered through chattering teeth.

He slipped his hand under the blanket. She was so chilled; he could feel it in the air trapped around her.

He headed to the bathroom. Stripping out of his clothes, he turned the shower on to the hottest temperature he could take as he soaped and rinsed off. Then he quickly dried himself, wrapping a towel around his middle.

At the bed, Colton dropped the towel as he lifted the bedclothes, sliding in beside Mya, covering her with his warmed body. She burrowed tight against him.

He was surprised how long it took before Mya was no longer cold. The old trope 'chilled to the bone' seemed to be fact for her today.

Finally, she eased away from him. "Thank you," she said as she maneuvered across the bed to get out on the other side. She headed to the closet; emerging in sweats. He automatically glanced at her feet. She was wearing a red and gray striped sock on it on one foot while a pink sock with white daisies was on her other.

She slipped out of the room and down the stairs. Rolling onto his back, Colton stared at the sky light. There was something so wrong between them. Instead of becoming closer, Mya was drawing farther and farther away from him. She never asked a single thing of him; not even to bring home something from the store. She was always tentative when it came to exhibiting affection outside of the gallery.

Actually, all she had ever asked was to be allowed to do the work she had been doing her whole life; well before he wandered through her door. And he so freakin' resented the space it could claim within her he had actually slapped her verbally yesterday. He closed his eyes. Something told him she would begin to hide her art; protecting it from any future judgment, which also meant she would be moving deeper into hiding from him. "So what's your next brilliant move, Williams?" he muttered.

He heard a yowl in reply. Cinnamon sat on the other side of the bed, staring at him. He reached out a hand. "I don't want to lose her either, Cin. Got any suggestions on what I should do?"

The cat yowled again.

"Sounds like good advice. Wish I understood what you were saying."

*****

When he came downstairs, Colton found Mya sitting in the middle of the kitchen floor, drying and putting her paint items back into the tote. She kept her eyes down as he crossed to the Keurig and brewed himself a cup of coffee.

Still not looking up, she said. "I don't want to live scared ever again, so please tell me what I did wrong yesterday that made you angry so I don't do it again."

Colton stared at her. Was he morphing into another Victor in her mind? Was that what last night all about? Protecting herself by tearing up her art to appease him? Staying on the streets for hours to keep out of harm's way? Maintaining a safe distance even in bed?

He backed away and headed for the porch. Of all the things he had been called by any woman, and some got pretty raunchy when he ended a relationship, abusive was not one of them. Why would Mya even think it? After all she was twenty-five. She had been in prior relationships.

His thoughts pulled up short. She had only been in two relationships. A dangerous one, where she had suffered god knows what at the hands of Victor, and theirs. And theirs hadn't been a model of trust and security, riddled as it was with his unjustified absenteeism prior to he and Cinnamon moving in.

He flashed to watching her get on the bus this morning, and not having any idea of where she was going. He suddenly realized he had not only not known, but he actually hadn't cared because she was just going to be painting windows; nothing that was real work like his job.

Right. He wasn't the one who had come home hypothermic from being out in the weather for hours. He hadn't put up with come-on comments and attitudes. He wasn't the one who had to make public transportation work for getting some place and, when it didn't, walking.

He was, in fact, dismissive of her whole professional life because everyone knew art wasn't important— except to lightweights like her and her friends.

And yet, there was a roof over his and Cin's head because of her 'lightweight efforts' for which she hadn't asked him to contribute one dime in the month they had lived there.

She was carrying it all while he thought he was being Mr. Commitment for pushing food at her now and again.

A nasty little voice threaded its way through the thoughts in his head. "You can always go home to your mother's. Pick up where you left off with women you understand instead of staying here and dealing with the artist."

"Did you really just think that," he said to himself. God, how he hated finding his mother's voice still crawled around in his brain, looking for places to rear its hateful head. But it suddenly threw light on something he was ignoring.

He was angry yesterday because he felt she had somehow violated her commitment to him, but he was definitely cutting deep corners in his to her.

"Steve told you to make the call, dude. Time to quit procrastinating. Either be the man Mya deserves or pack your shit and get out of her life permanently." Entering the gallery, he looked around and realized just how quickly he could be packed and out of the door. He climbed up to the second floor. On the other side of the wall, Mya was sitting in the fading light from the window, sketching in one of her books. Cin was sitting next to her, pawing at her hair where it fell over her shoulder onto the floor.

As he watched her silently, he found clarity in his position. He would have absolutely no problem walking away from her—if his very next action was to put a real bullet through his brain because it would be the only way he would never think of her again. Time to cut the bullcrap and go all in.

As he started crossing to her, Mya looked up and quickly hid her sketchbook behind her. He held out his hand. She hesitated before taking it; keeping her eyes warily on him.

Pulling her to her feet, he led her to the bedroom. Once they were beside the bed, he patted it. "Sit down, baby," he said.

He squatted down in front of her. "Mya, please believe me when I tell you I will never lift a hand to you or physically hurt you, no matter what you do. I have been known to yell and when really pushed to the edge, I have punched a wall or two, but I never have and never will strike a woman, especially if the woman is you."

He ran his hand down the side of her face. "It kills me you are afraid of me. I am not Victor."

Mya's eyes widened when he said the man's name. "How…"

"Nancy told me a while back. And I guess I behaved yesterday in ways which somehow made you think I was turning into… that bastard." He paused, lowering his head before looking back at her. "When I got home yesterday, you looked like you had been making love to someone while I was gone. You had the same beautiful glow I see after we have loved."

Mya sucked in her breath sharply. "I wouldn't…," she whispered.

"I know, but logic is not the first place a man goes when certain parts of his life are seemingly violated. Even when I saw no evidence, I still couldn't shake the feeling you had somehow cheated on me."

Mya turned her head away. His betrayal was clear in her expression and body language.

He put his hand out to turn her face back to him. "Mya, living with you is like living with a beautiful, sexy alien. You pop off to places I can't see, and I can never track what suddenly called you away. Yesterday, you were someone I didn't even know existed. Nancy said you were Mya in Ecstasy— yes, I called her because I was so confused at what was happening with you.

"I screwed up big time yesterday. I acted like all your beautiful work was some kind of stupid insult to my cat because I was angry about something I couldn't even name, but I absolutely never meant for you to destroy it. Baby, I know jack shit about art so you must understand two things. One, you do not need my permission to do anything your heart and soul needs to do and two, you must never destroy anything you do again because of me and my big mouth. I may bitch, but I will survive if once in while I have to take the back-seat to your work. Understand?"

He watched her face carefully as she nodded. There was uncertainty, but the fear was dissipating, although caution crept back in when he said, "There's one more thing.

"Baby, I need you to use me." Colton gave a sudden grin. "For more than just my body, anyway."

She ducked her head as a smile slipped across her lips.

"I need you to ask me to do things, fix things, stop for things from the store on my way home, take out the garbage, pick my own damn clothes up off the floor. Call me on my cell phone and demand to know where I'm at and what time I'll be home… I don't care what. Just start building some dependency on me, please. Otherwise, I'm going to live every day convinced I will come home from work and find Cin and my stuff parked out by the sidewalk."

"I would never dump Cinnamon" she said as she leaned forward to put her arms around his neck, nearly falling off the bed. Throwing himself forward to catch her, they both fell back on the bed.

His kiss became suggestive as his hand began to roam. Mya caught it. "Huh-huh, you had your chance earlier." She pushed out from under him.

"You were an ice cube," he countered as he sat up. "Do you have any idea what ice cubes do to man parts?"

"Well, this ice cube is starving. So please feed me," she said as she headed to the closet to change. Colton took them to Cactus Flats where they demolished a large nacho. Then he headed a few blocks over to Railey's Outdoor Store.

"Do you need something?" Mya asked as she unfastened her seatbelt.

He waited until she was out of the truck. "No. But you do," he said, taking her arm and steering her in the direction of the store.

She tried to turn back to the truck. "I can't afford Railey's," she said.

"I can," he said. "We're getting you proper gear to wear when you window paint. I don't ever again want to see you as cold and wet as you were today. It's not the way a man takes care of the woman he loves." He pulled her in under his arm where gratifyingly she leaned slightly into him.

*****

Over the next couple of weeks, Colton learned the confidence he had wanted Mya to feel in their relationship was not happening as smoothly and easily as he might have wished for. While she made conscious attempts to try to meet his requests, she more frequently fell into her autonomous patterns. And, although she had rarely shown him her creations in the earlier part of their relationship, she was even more careful to not share her work with him now. He got it. If someone had kicked Cinnamon, he would have made sure his cat was where it could never happen again, but when she hid away in her upstairs work space, he found he was lonely for her presence. Even Cin seemed to prefer to hang out with her.

Chapter 26

When the night of the youth center preview arrived, Mya wore the same dress and shoes she had worn when they went to the Caverns. Watching her come down the stairs carrying her jean jacket, scarf, and portfolio, Colton realized he was just as stunned by her as he had been the first time.

At the truck, he took her portfolio and placed it on the seat before again telling her to face him so he could lift her in. She hesitated. "Hmmm, this is feeling like last time and last time I didn't see you again for two months."

He bent over and scooped her up in his arms. "I have to come back. All my underwear is here now," he said as he kissed her and set her in the seat.

She smiled back at him. "That is not reassuring. You go commando."

*****

The parking around the youth center was jammed with expensive vehicles. "Who should we offend by parking next to?" Colton asked. He glanced at Mya when he didn't get a response; noticing she was rubbing her hands over her skirt. It took a moment, but then he thought of the incongruity of her being invited to view a building containing someone else's artwork.

He pulled into a space between an Audi and a Lexus, and switched off the engine. Turning in his seat, he reached for her hands. "You do not have to do this if you don't want to. I'm sure

135

Wally and Nancy would completely understand."

Mya shook her head. "No. I'm probably being totally masochistic, but I would like to see what was done with the walls. And Nancy asked me to bring my portfolio because there were a couple of people who are supposed to be here tonight who might be interested in commissioning some work."

After lifting her down from the truck, Colton wrapped his arms around her. "When you're ready, just say the word, baby, and we can be out of here and slumming over a beer at the Sellah in a heartbeat."

She held onto him for a moment. Then lifting her head off his shoulder, she squared her shoulders. "Show time."

Wally and Nancy were standing at the entrance greeting people. Nancy hugged Mya, whispering in her ear. "It's beyond awful. The Board is absolutely pissed and Mr. Moneybags' daughter is so clueless she is wandering around handing out business cards to do commissioned work. It's an effin' disaster."

Inside the art was worse than even Mya could have imagined. The colors were all drab ochres, olives, greys, and eggplant. The walls were smeared with grotesquely distorted animal shapes, and a lot of random unidentifiable shapes. The whole thing looked like it had been slapped up hastily; the brush stokes uneven and sloppy.

Colton put his hand on the back of Mya's neck and squeezed. It was horrible to look at for someone who knew nothing about art. It must be absolutely killing Mya who had presented beautiful ideas, and had the chops to execute them, to see what she had been replaced with.

When she turned to look at him he could see the distress in her eyes. She leaned in. 'This is so unfair to Wally and Nancy. Any kids showing up here will be absolutely traumatized by these walls."

Just then a voice boomed through the room. "What the hell happened here? I thought we contracted with an artist, not the punks who spray paint graffiti over at the old Timm's warehouse."

Mya closed her eyes. She knew the voice well.

A red-faced stocky man in an expensive suit stomped angrily into the room. "Who is talking about my daughter like that?" he bellowed.

Jack Parker stood dead center in the room, fists on his hips as he surveyed the debacle spread across the wall.

The man stopped abruptly when Jack's icy blue gaze focused on him. He started to explain. "Well, my daughter likes to mess around with art sometimes and since I was kicking in some pretty big bucks, I thought she deserved the contract instead of the other person."

Jack crossed his arms over his chest and looked down at the shorter man. "Oh, you mean the other person who actually followed the protocol the Board, which included you, set out for soliciting and awarding the contract to do the wall art? The other person who might have had expectations the Board would actually stand by its contractual obligation? The other person who might even sue us for breach of contract? That other person, Brad?"

"The Board didn't breach the contract, Jack. We withdrew it through an amendment we voted on."

"Sorry but I don't remember it coming up at the last Board meeting."

"I...er...called a special meeting when my daughter told me she wanted to do the art."

"Funny, I don't remember being notified about a special meeting."

"I had a quorum," the man said defensively.

"I bet you did and I bet they are all really proud they backed you based on what they're seeing now."

Several people scurried into other rooms and a woman who looked to be slightly older than Mya ran sobbing in the direction of the restrooms.

*****

Colton looked at Mya. She shrugged. "Vintage Dad."

"Sounds like he was standing up for you though."

She shook her head. "It isn't about me. I doubt Dad even remembers who the original contract was awarded to. Dad just hates it when he thinks someone has cut him out of control by going around him."

Nancy came up. "You can always count on Jack to come straight to the point. I can't wait for the next Board meeting. It is going to be a doozy. And, Colton, may I borrow your lady for a few minutes. I have someone who wants to see her portfolio." She pointed down the hall. "There is food and drink in the gym area. I know you know where it is."

Colton watched as Nancy and Mya crossed the room, heading into what he remembered to be the conference room before he turned towards the gym. A redhead sheathed in sequins watched him pass, and pursing her lips in appreciation, followed.

Several long tables were spread with a variety of food together with other smaller tables arranged for seating. Standing at the end of one, holding a loaded plate, was Duncan. He waved a shrimp at Colton.

"So where's Mya?" he asked as he dipped the shrimp in cocktail sauce and popped it into his mouth.

"Nancy lined up a couple of people who wanted to see her portfolio for possible commissions. She's with one of them now."

A lovely black woman came up and affectionately patted Duncan's stomach. "Finish filling it up, baby. We have about twenty minutes left before the tanks overflow and I need to pump."

Duncan dipped and gave her a bite of a shrimp. "Hon, this is Colton. We worked together on this building. He is also a friend of Mya's."

She held her hand out as a twinkle came into her eyes. "Perhaps a bit more than just a friend," she said. "At least according those of us who spend our time getting all up in each other's business."

Colton glanced away sheepishly.

"I forgot to warn you, man. Your lady, my wife, and Nancy have never taken a single breath without the other knowing about it. I swear Nancy and Mya called Anita to congratulate her on being pregnant before I had finished doing my part."

"Women just know things," Anita said.

"Huh-huh. I think you three share the same brain," he answered. "You know way too much about each other. It scares Wally and me, and now that Colton is in the family, he'll learn to be scared, too, whenever the three of you are in the same vicinity."

When Anita moved off to talk to another couple, Colton asked about Duncan's 'Cool Train' schedule.

"Right now Cool Train is pretty much parked at the station, other than a few stray private gigs I contracted for before Penny arrived. Damn, man, you want to turn your world inside out? Have a baby. The minute she slid into this world, she had me by the heart. What I didn't realize was those itty bitty hands were grabbing my life by the balls and twisting every single thing in it around to suit her convenience.

"It wasn't too bad the first couple of months because Anita was on maternity leave. But she went back to teaching fulltime this fall. Now we're juggling nannies, breast pumping, night feedings. Thank god for Mya, Shonda, and Monique. They are always willing to jump in and give Anita and me a few baby-free hours.

"But you know what's really pathetic? You head out the door eager for a baby break, then you spend your whole time talking about the baby, and after about ninety minutes, you can hardly wait to get home and see what's doing with the baby."

Duncan shook his head at the vagaries of parenthood and changed the subject. "So what project you working on now?"

The two men discussed work until Anita returned to collect Duncan. She gave Colton a hug. "Tell Mya to call me and that I love her."

"I will," he promised as he shook Duncan's hand. "Take care."

Colton turned toward the beverage table to get a cup of coffee when he was intercepted by the redhead. "So what's your name," she asked, striking a seductive pose.

"Colton," he said cautiously.

"Hmmmm. That's a nice name. I'm Claire. This seems like an odd place for a guy like you to be hanging out."

"I'm with someone."

She reached for his left hand and ran her finger- tips over his ring finger. "It doesn't look serious," she said with a suggestive side-eye glance.

His impulse was to yank his hand away. Instead, he gritted his teeth and slowly extricated it from her grasp. She moved in closer. He backed up. Before she could move in again, Mya stepped between them. She smiled sweetly as she held her hand out. "Hello. I'm Mya Parker. I see you have met Colton already."

The female took a big step back. "Mya Parker? Are you related to Jack?"

"I'm his daughter."

Pivoting on her high heel, the woman bolted. Colton watched the woman swiftly vanish through the door into the hall. "How did you know?"

"She came with dad? Do you see anyone else dressed like a stripper here?"

"So how did it go?" Colton asked as he touched her portfolio.

"Nothing is promised but if it works out, it might be up to six wall hangings for a private music school. Of course, I have to draw up the designs in order to get approval." Her blue eyes glowed with her excitement at the prospect.

They turned when Mya heard her name called again. Nancy was motioning to her. "I'll be back. Try to stay out of trouble this time."

He gave her a quick kiss on the cheek. "No promises."

He watched her cross to the door, disappearing through it with Nancy. He jumped when a deep voice spoke behind him.

"She is just as beautiful as her mother was."

Colton spun around to see Jack looking down at him.

He extended his hand. "Jack Parker. And you are Colton Williams, the man who is sharing my daughter's bed, right?"

Colton flushed deeply. "How did you know?"

"While I'm pretty sure my daughter has told you I wouldn't be able to pick her out of a lineup of one, it isn't entirely true."

"Actually, Mya hasn't said anything about you. She tends to stay silent on a lot of things."

Jack nodded. "She gets that from her mother. Abigail would never say anything to me she thought would upset or stress me. It's why she didn't tell me she had cut her foot on some rusted metal at the house we were remodeling until I woke up to find her on fire with fever beside me. Thirty-six hours later she was dead from sepsis." He paused. "Mya was eight months old."

Colton looked at Jack. The pain on his face still looked fresh.

"So what do you do for a living, Williams?"

Something told Colton Jack already knew the answer to his question. "I'm in construction. I worked on this project and I'm currently on the hardware store remodel over on Farmington Road."

"You any good with general handyman stuff—you know, minor electrical, plumbing, general repairs, yardwork?"

"Yeah. My dad died when I was thirteen and it kinda fell to me to learn to do stuff for my mom."

Jack pulled a card case out of his pocket. "So are you paying her bills while she spends the day finger painting?"

Colton bristled. "No, sir. She is paying everything out of the money she earns with her art. She works long hours and damn hard for every dime, but she won't accept anything from me to help cover costs, even though I'm living there. She said it's her responsibility, not mine, to keep a roof over her head."

Jack smiled. "I taught her that. I didn't ever want her to rely on somebody who could leave her high and dry one day."

"That may have been your intent, Mr. Parker, but what she really learned is she isn't worth anyone caring about," Colton replied softly.

Jack studied Colton for a moment as he tapped the card he had pulled out against his thumb nail before handing it to Colton. "If you're interested, I'm looking for someone to oversee my commercial rental properties. Do minor repairs. Clean and prep them for renting when vacant, hire contractors when necessary, show them, etc. I'll pay you twenty-five percent more than you're earning now to start with. Get your property management license and I'll raise it. Let me know." Jack started toward the door.

"You know it was Mya who lost the contract to do the art in here, don't you?" Colton said.

Jack turned back; his face grim. "I sure as hell do." He looked directly into Colton's eyes. "It's not smart to hurt my baby in any way. There will be payback. No exceptions. Understand?"

Colton watched the man stride towards the hall. And, although the evidence pointed in a different direction, he recognized Jack Parker probably genuinely loved his daughter in his own way.

Colton slipped the card Jack had given him into the breast pocket of his jean jacket before Mya returned

Chapter 27

They could have driven right to the Sellah, but Mya pleaded for them to park in front of the gallery and walk over in the misty rain sifting gently from the sky. When Colton lifted her down from the truck, she undid the clasp holding her hair, shaking it loose, before turning her face up to the soft wetness. The slight tension visible in her face relaxed.

"Tonight smells so wonderfully October," she said as she drew in a deep breath.

"I didn't know October had a smell," he said as he locked and closed the truck door.

"It's smoky offerings and sacrificial leaves; dark moons and ancient dreams; sighing spirits and sad death."

Her words unsettled Colton. Looking at her he saw she had her head slightly turned and her lips were parted like she was listening to whispers carried in the wind. A strange feeling crawled up his spine. It made him turn his own eyes to peer into the shadows. Then something pressed lightly against the side of his throat. Colton smiled down at her. He adored the unexpected touch of her lips on various parts of his body.

"I think the word was beer?" she said.

He wrapped his arm around her shoulders, pulling her against him. "Beer it was."

Jake had just removed the remains of a totcho from the table and replaced Colton's empty with a fresh glass of beer when Colton reached into his pocket and pulled out the card Jack had given him at the youth center.

"Your dad offered me a job tonight," he said as he held the card out to Mya.

Mya looked startled. 'I didn't know you knew dad."

"I don't, but he knew my name and that I was, ahem, sharing his daughter's bed."

Mya took the card and stared at it wistfully. "He probably learned it from Duncan. Duncan does a lot of work for dad. So what job did he offer you?"

"To help with his commercial rental properties; you know, handle repairs, clean-up, maintenance, and showing vacancies. He offered me twenty-five percent more than I'm earning now, and, if I was to get my property manager license, he would give me even more."

Mya looked at him. "Is it something you would like to do?"

"It feels like it might have more potential than just sawing boards and pounding nails for the rest of my life."

Mya nodded. "It definitely would. My dad is very generous with his knowledge of real estate and property, and he has got a ton of it. He loves mentoring people interested in that stuff. He did a lot of it until—," she stopped and bit her lip.

Colton squeezed her hand. "Victor," he said.

"Yeah. I guess I kinda screwed the whole thing up." She handed the card back and smiled at him. "I think it is an amazing opportunity for you if it is what you want. Just watch out for his skanks."

Colton looked uncomfortable. "I really don't know why they feel they have to hit on somebody else when they are with your dad."

"Not 'somebody else'... you." Reaching her hand out, she lightly traced his jaw line with her fingertips. "Have you ever looked at yourself in the mirror? They are attracted to Dad's power and money, but what they really want is to crawl into bed with is someone who is devastatingly handsome and virile. And that would be you."

He kissed her fingers when they drifted over his mouth. "Absolutely not available or interested."

Even as she smiled, something was still sinking inside of her. Her dad was powerful, charismatic, and had a way of absorbing everyone around him into his personal sphere. Once they were in, it was all about him with outside distractions definitely discouraged.

Her eyes rested on Colton's face. She had always assumed she would lose Colton, but to another woman; someone more beautiful, talented, sexier, whatever. She did not expect she might lose him to her own father. But her dad had the gift of helping other people come into their own. She could not; would not deny Colton that.

*****

In the night she dreamed of her father and Colton. They were surrounded by beautiful young women with big busts spilling out of short dresses. Everyone was getting into a huge limousine. When she got to the vehicle's door, her dad said, "Sorry, Mya, there's no room for you." The door swung closed and it pulled away, leaving her standing in the road alone.

She threw her hand out as she awoke with a gasp. He was still there, sleeping beside her. She turned and crawled into his arms.

"Baby?" Colton murmured sleepily.

"Please, just hold me," she whispered

Chapter 28

Colton called the number on the card Jack had given him. Jack's secretary answered the phone. Advised Mr. Parker was out, he left the message he would like to accept the employment offered the previous evening, if it was still available.

Just before lunch, Gary came up to him. "So this is your last day on the crew, huh."

Colton looked at him perplexed.

"I just got a call from the general contractor who said you were going to work for Mr. Parker doing something else starting Monday so today was it for you."

"He offered me a job in his property management and I called to let him know I was going to take it if it was available, but he hasn't actually talked to me and I was going to give you two weeks' notice."

"Well, it sounds like you got the job, and since this is a Parker project, he has the right to yank you without even thirty seconds notice. Congratulations."

At noon, Colton checked his cell phone and found a text message advising him Mr. Parker would meet with him Monday at the property management office to review the details of his employment and outline his duties. He suddenly felt nervous. It was one thing to think about Jack Parker as Mya's missing in action dad and the name of the person whose construction projects he worked on. It was going to be another to be more directly involved in his businesses.

At the end of the day, he gathered up his personal tools and loaded them in the truck. A couple of the crew who had worked with him on other projects stopped to shake his hand. Then he was driving away from the only work life he had known since he was sixteen years old.

*****

Monday morning, Mya was waiting with Colton's travel mug of coffee. She had a small blank sketchbook and pen in her hands.

When Colton came into the kitchen, she handed them to him. "I'm not sure whether you'll really be meeting Dad today or not, but if so, this will help. Dad loves it when people take the time to actually write notes down," she said. "It will also help because Dad tends to subject-hop so trying to remember stuff later can be tough. Also, Dad doesn't remember other people get hungry at meal time. When he's involved he forgets to eat. If you happen to be with him at lunch, offer to take him out for a quick burger or something. He's not fussy."

Colton's eyes were impish as he shot her a look.

"Yeah, yeah. It runs in the family. Don't be afraid to ask questions or seek clarification. Dad's philosophy is the only dumb question is the one that isn't asked."

"Anything else?" Colton asked.

Crossing her arms over her chest, Mya looked down and drew a breath before looking at him. "I'm the one subject Dad doesn't want to hear anything about so while you're on the time clock, I don't exist—to him or anyone else who works there." She leaned in and kissed him. "You are going to do great and Dad is so going to be bragging about what a genius he was to hire you before the end of the week."

*****

Although Colton was generally punctual, he arrived ten minutes earlier per Mya's recommendation. As he pulled into the parking lot dominated by a sign saying Parker's Premier Properties – Commercial, someone wearing a dark coat with a hood was in the process of unlocking the door.

Colton parked, and grabbing the sketchbook and coffee, followed. Surprisingly when he stepped inside he didn't see anyone although the coat was now hung on a coat tree.

"Hello?"

A door opened and a woman, who would have been labeled on the construction site as 'stacked', stepped out of the rest room. She was wearing black boots which came to the middle of her thighs and a tight black sweater dress short enough to reveal skin between it and the boots. Her hair fell to her mid-back, although the blonde color looked like it originated in a bottle.

Upon seeing him, she did the all too familiar slow look-over, before flashing a smile which was a combination of welcome and 'come on'. "Can I help you?"

"I'm supposed to meet Mr. Parker here."

Before she could answer, the door behind Colton opened and Jack stepped through.

The day became a blur as Jack first gave Colton a tour of all the properties which would be his responsibility from the seat of his Mercedes. They included professional buildings, a couple of small strip malls, a storage unit site, and a couple of individual locations.

He then led him through the systems established to ensure maintenance was done in a timely manner, the reporting of problems by renters, purchasing of materials and supplies, and lists of approved contractors for large or complex problems.

Colton learned the woman in the office was Chaileen and she handled all the paperwork. Under Jack's watchful eye, she showed him the protocols for providing her with receipts, project forms, contractor bids, and completing his time sheets for allocation of costs.

By the end of the day, Colton had the keys to a fully outfitted service truck, credits cards for fuel and to use for necessary materials and supplies, master keys to all the properties, as well as the property management office, a property management dedicated cell phone, and Mya's sketchbook full of notes.

Jack left after having Colton sign various employment related documents. "Your hours are eight to six with an hour for lunch and a couple of breaks whenever you want them, although you're on call 24/7 so you might be pulling a few extra hours here or there. Glad to have you on board."

Then Jack was out the door and, in a moment, out of the parking lot.

Colton watched him leave with a bemused expression. He had just spent almost ten hours with the man, much of it without an audience, and Jack had never once asked about his daughter or even referenced her.

He glanced at the clock when Chaileen shut off her computer and started to gather up her coat and purse. It was just a few minutes before six.

"You know, I've worked here for seven years now and you must be like the tenth guy who has been hired for the job, and although Jack has shown up to do the glad-hand thing, he has never provided the orientation like he did for you today, so I guess you're somebody special, right?"

Colton shook his head. "No. Not special."

"Well, that's your story. Congratulations, you have now completed your first day," as she glanced over her shoulder at the clock on the wall. "How about we go someplace for a drink?"

"Thank you, but I need to get home."

"Got somebody already?"

"Yes."

Chaileen shrugged. "Too bad. Maybe you'll want to trade up someday."

Colton let the comment blow by him as he followed her out. He waited until she had locked the door and went to her car. He crossed to his truck once he observed her safely inside it.

She noted his actions. "Oh, yeah, beautiful man. Whatever you have waiting at home is going to be nowhere as interesting as what's going to be waiting for you here at work. You are so going to be in my bed by Christmas. It'll be my present to me... and you."

Chapter 29

Mya was upstairs working when Colton came through the door. She beelined for the downstairs when she heard the door open and close; stopping at the bottom of the stairs to scrutinize him.

"Okay?" she asked.

He smiled. "Yeah, although I feel like someone threw me in the deep end of the pool. Almost ten hours of orientation with your dad is pretty intense."

"Dad oriented you?"

"Yes. The office gal said it was the first time she had seen him do it in all the years she had been there."

"I have never known Dad to do it either. I think you may be what Dad has been wanting forever."

"What's that?"

"The son he missed out on when he ended up with me." She gave a quiet smile. "My dad has his issues, but he's basically a good person. Maybe he could make up a little for the father you were cheated out of as well."

Colton stared at her. She had the most unsettling ability to reach inside him and put light on something painful he refused to even acknowledge.

They heard her phone begin to ring. Mya scampered up the stairs, climbing back down them with her phone to her ear.

"Let me ask," she said. "Wally and Nancy are wondering if it would be alright to drop by. They promise they are bearing food and booze."

Colton shrugged. "Sure."

"That's a go, girl. See you in a few."

151

She clicked off, as she passed by on her way to the kitchen. She returned a minute later with a beer, holding it out to him. He took it and set it on the counter. "I need this more," he said as he pulled her in for a long kiss.

Abruptly, he let go and grabbed for his mid-section. "Oooow." Pulling his shirt up, several tiny dots of blood appeared on his side. Cinnamon yowled petulantly from her position on the counter.

Grabbing the tail of the tank top she was wearing under one of Colton's old Henleys, Mya reached out and dabbed off the blood before bending over to kiss the place. "That's what you get for not keeping your priorities straight on who is the main chick and who is the side chick here," she said with a grin.

The door behind them opened, and Nancy leaned in. "Kinky, guys. You want us to leave and come back later?"

"Nah, just mopping up the aftermath of a cat fight for a gorgeous man's attention," Mya said.

Nancy pushed through with two large pizza boxes in her hand. Wally was right behind with a short case of beer and three folding lawn chairs he was carrying. He handed the beer off to Colton as he came through the door.

"I really appreciate your ability to live Mya's zen lifestyle, but the floor just doesn't do it for me," Wally said as he began to open the chairs.

Colton followed the women who had disappeared into the kitchen with the pizza.

"So how was your first day in Parkerland?" Nancy asked as she and Mya pulled plates from the cupboard.

"A little overwhelming. Jack's a pretty focused guy."

Nancy lifted her eyebrow. "Jack?"

"Yeah. Dad gave Colton his orientation today," Mya clarified.

Nancy turned appraising eyes on Colton. "Seriously? Interesting."

A weird vibe passed through Colton. He wondered if he should be concerned about the fact everyone viewed Jack's time with him today as extremely unusual.

The subject changed to food when Nancy flipped opened the lids of the two boxes. "And tonight, for your dining pleasure, we have the Gatling and the Bonnie and Clyde."

In minutes the foursome were settling in the open space. Wally, Nancy, and Colton in the chairs while Mya and the cat shared the counter top. Conversation was minimal as pizza was devoured and beer drunk. Mya shared bits of sausage and pepperoni with Cinnamon.

Finally, Colton collected plates and brought fresh beer back for him and Wally. Wally took a sip before leaning forward.

"We need to bring you up to date on what's been happening at the center since last Thursday's unveiling of the worst excuse for art in the history of the world.

"Friday morning, Jack sent over a team of painters to cover the mess. And Friday afternoon, Brad showed up with a check to repay what had been allocated to cover the costs of wall art. So as of this moment, we have fresh clean walls and no art." He took another swallow.

"Now, here's the situation. The Board reinstated your contract to do the art based on what was accepted last summer, but the Center officially opened today and we already have kids utilizing the building. So, we need a plan on how you can do this around the center's schedule which is six a.m. to eight p.m."

Mya sat very still as the information sank in. Colton, Nancy, and Wally exchanged glances. Knowing Mya as well as they did, they knew this was her way of absorbing and dealing with it. Abruptly, she turned her head slightly away from them while her eyes studied nothing they could see.

"And there she goes," Nancy said quietly.

In a minute, Mya scrambled off the counter and dashed upstairs. She came back down with a sketchbook and drawing pencil; resuming her cross-legged position on the counter. The pencil began to move over the page. She stopped and stared at it for a moment, then set her pencil down and turned the page toward the others.

"Maybe this would work. Instead of painting directly on the walls, how about painting a wall sized canvas and hanging it? I could do the painting here, then it could be hung. Also, if you decided to change the use of the rooms around, you would just have to move the canvasses."

Wally got out of his chair to lean over her shoulder. "How would we hang it?"

"Grommets at the top to slip over a rod or hooks, and then," she pointed with her pencil tip, "a small pocket at the bottom filled with sand or something similar to keep it from floating, but would be safe if a kid fell into it."

"How much canvas are we talking about?"

"I have the original measurements upstairs," Mya said as she slid off the counter. Wally followed her.

"So how is it going?" Nancy asked Colton as soon as the two were safely upstairs.

He shrugged. "She's a challenge. I just wish I could get her to need me more."

"Trust me, she needs you." He shot her a skeptical look.

"Colton, Jack raised Mya to be self-sufficient, self-reliant, and self-contained. I think he thought he was giving her tools she would need to survive in case... I don't know... something happened to him. Unfortunately, he did such a good job it is actually incomprehensible to her to look to anyone else for anything. It's like to do that would be to admit some kind of weakness or failing."

"You know she won't let me help with any of the expenses here. The most I am allowed to do is buy a few groceries now and then and pay for dinner when we go out."

"I suspected as much. And let me guess, she won't ask you for any help or to do stuff around here either."

He shook his head. "I am bad about dropping my clothes wherever I take them off. She just picks them up instead demanding I put them where they belong."

Nancy looked down and smiled. Colton didn't know it, but that was Wally's modus operandi, too.

"I've asked her to make demands on me so I feel like I matter in her life."

Nancy reached out and squeezed Colton's arm. "Please don't doubt how much you matter in her life." She glanced towards the upstairs. "I had actually begun to believe after the whole Victor thing Mya would never open herself to the possibility of a relationship again. For five years, she wouldn't even go to coffee with a guy." She smiled warmly. "The fact she let you through her door and ultimately into her life says volumes about you, and her need for you."

Wally and Mya came back down the stairs. Mya was talking. "We can use just regular painter canvases like I showed you. You can get them at any hardware store. Same thing with the grommets. They usually come with a tool for setting them. Sand, primer, sealer, and the paint and we should be good to go."

"So how about I pick you up tomorrow and we go shopping?" Wally asked.

Mya shook her head. "I have some windows tomorrow, but maybe I can come by the center when I'm done?"

Wally and Nancy began to gather things up to go. Wally caught Colton's brief look of regret as he folded the chairs. He handed the best of them to him. "Just in case you are a little tired of the floor being your main seating." Colton grinned his appreciation as he tucked it in the storage area under the stairs.

Colton showered and crawled into the bed while Mya completed the locking up. She smiled when she got to the bedroom and saw he had already fallen asleep. She turned off the reading light on his side before circling back and slipping under the covers.

Sensing her, he reached out, wrapping an arm over her waist. He pulled her tight against him, even as his soft, slow breath against her hair told her he had not wakened. For one moment, she allowed herself to feel loved.

*****

Starting with his second day, Colton began to establish a routine for himself. He addressed requests for repairs before parceling out regular maintenance duties, and ending the day with providing necessary paperwork to Chaileen. Although she refrained from solicitous comments, she used every opportunity to convey her interest in him through suggestive body language.

When six o'clock arrived, he was in the process of determining his plan for the next day. Chaileen came over and leaned against his desk.

"I can stay if you want me to," she said.

Colton looked at her with a cool expression. "No need. I'm good." He kept his eyes focused on her until she moved away to gather her coat and purse. Outside the door, she gave a pleasurable little twitch of her shoulders. It was boring when guys would drop into her bed with only minimal effort on her part. It was much more rewarding when she had to work at convincing them she was the prize they wanted.

*****

The display pedestals had been moved out of the gallery and were arranged in the space behind the counter when Colton got home. A glance in the gallery showed a pile of packaged canvasses, a couple of tarps, a small bag of sand, and a several boxes filled with paint and brushes neatly lined up under the window overlooking the porch.

He heard noise in the kitchen and headed there. Mya had a pan on the stove and was setting the little table.

She smiled. "I'm cooking dinner."

He crossed to the stove to see hot dogs boiling in water. Looking back at her, she had the same proud look small children wear when they are have accomplished something they thought might be beyond their ken.

"Yes, you are," he answered as he reached out for her. When she was inside his arms, he could not imagine anyone more adorable existed anywhere. "God, I love you," he whispered in her ear.

Chapter 30

By Friday, Colton felt like he was beginning to gain a little bit of a hand hold in his new job. Additionally, he was able to deflect Chaileen's subtle maneuvers by heading out in the service truck almost as soon as he clocked in and returning late in the day.

He was just securing the service truck when Jack pulled into the parking lot. Following him into the building, Jack motioned to him. "Finish what you need to do."

Colton headed to his desk and stapled a couple of receipts to job orders. He replaced a couple of keys in the secured master box, and then signed his time sheet before putting all the paperwork in the appropriate basket on Chaileen's desk.

"Done?" Jack asked. Colton nodded.

"Then, how about a drink with me at O'Boye's? We can ride over in my car."

"If you don't mind, I would just as soon meet you there so you wouldn't have to bring me back to get my truck."

"That works. See you there in a few."

Once in his truck, he quickly texted Mya to tell her Jack had invited him for drinks. "Should I be nervous?"

She texted back. "No. Dad only has drinks with women he wants to sleep with or people he wants to do business with. You're good."

When Colton's beer and Jack's whiskey on the rocks were in front of them, Jack took a sip before leaning back. "Have you given any thought to getting your property manager license?"

Colton shook his head. "Not really, sir. I'm still trying to get a good handle on what I'm supposed to be doing for you now."

"The reports to me say you are doing a fine job." Jack caught Colton's raised eyebrow. "I didn't get where I am by not keeping track of what's happening. Everything crosses my desk so I called and talked with a couple of the businesses you had done work at."

Jack took another sip of his whiskey. "I've spent the last quarter century building my business, but now I have grown it to where it is becoming more and more difficult for me to stay on top of all the parts. It's been a goal of mine to find someone who could take on more of the day to day management stuff, freeing me up to concentrate on the big picture, and," he winked at Colton, "maybe sneak in some more golf.

"I had a guy a few years back I was thinking might be a fit. Unfortunately," Jack paused to sip again.

"He liked to beat women?" Colton asked.

Jack threw a sharp look at him. "Mya tell you?"

Colton shook his head. "Nancy. Thanks for saving her."

For a brief moment, Jack's face was grave. "She had so many bruises, and she never said anything. Just hid it all… to protect what she thought I wanted."

Bruises weren't the only damage she hid from you, Colton thought. "You wouldn't happen to know where he is because I would very much like to return the favor." While his tone sounded mild, there was an ugly harshness in Colton's eyes and expression indicating the threat was not idle.

And that gave Jack the last piece he was looking for. Colton had a vein of dark anger in him. He was a man who would only be pushed so far before he pushed back—hard.

Jack concluded the conversation by taking a bathroom break. On his way to the men's room, he noted Chaileen sitting at the bar staring at their table. She had her eyes so focused on Colton's back, she didn't even notice his six foot three frame crossing the room.

On his return trip, Jack leaned in, startling her. "Got the hots for the new guy, huh?"

She shrugged. "So?"

"He's off-limits, Chaileen."

"Says who?"

"Me. The man who signs your pay checks. You want to keep them coming, you stick to business in the office and stay away the rest of the time. Capiche?"

She stared after him as he continued on to the table. Who was this guy? First, Jack orients him personally; now he's buying him drinks and telling her to keep her distance or look for new work.

Jack sat down at the table and looked directly at her. She swallowed the last of her drink, slipped on her coat, and left.

Jack may think he is controlling the game but he had just taken it to a whole new level of challenge she thought as she headed for her car.

Chapter 31

It was after nine when Colton pushed into the gallery bearing a bag of tacos. Mya was on her knees outlining a design on a primed canvas. As she edged her way off, he was waiting with an outstretched hand to bring her to her feet and into his arms; Jack's words 'so many bruises' at the forefront of his mind.

She leaned back. "So, what was dear old pater about?"

Keeping hold of her hand, he pulled her toward the kitchen, grabbing the bag off the counter as he went by.

"So Dad wants you to take the classes in order to get your property manager license, and then start assuming some of his duties so he has more free time to golf and chase skanks."

Colton reached across the table to wipe a bit of taco sauce from the corner of her mouth. "He left out the skanks part."

"When you get your license, is he expecting you to keep up with what you're doing now as well?"

"No. He said we'll hire someone else to take my place and I will move over to his office."

"And it's a ten week course at six hours a week?"

"Well, since it doesn't start until the second week of November, it is actually going to be a twelve week course because of the holidays and review day before the licensing test. I just hope I can do it. It's been a while since I had to hit the books and I wasn't exactly great when I did."

"My dad wouldn't be offering you this opportunity unless he thought you had what it takes. Trust him. He will not let you fail."

Colton looked at her sweet, serious face and thought how strange her words were. She hadn't trusted her dad to care even when some

161

asshole was regularly beating the shit out of her, and, yet, she was saying Jack definitely could be counted on to have his back.

Mya picked several bits of meat off the taco wrapper and fed then to Cinnamon who was sitting at her feet before scrunching it up to toss in the bag. She got up to make herself a cup of tea; stopping at the refrigerator on her way back to the table to bring him a beer. She had just handed it over when her phone chimed indicating she had a message.

She was reading it as she returned from the gallery room. She quickly typed back an answer. "I need to go to Steve and Kelly's tomorrow to see what she has in the way of batik fabric. We were just clarifying times between bus and nap schedules," she said as she sat back down at the table.

"Tomorrow is Saturday, you know."

Mya looked confused. "Yes, but the flea market is closed until March."

"Baby, I don't work tomorrow. You do not need to worry about catching the bus because I can take you any time you need to go." He could tell by her expression it had never occurred to her to ask him for a ride.

After living with a mother who had always treated him as a personal minion and being in relationships in which it was presumed he was there to fulfil the other person's every want or need, it was sometimes unmanning to live in the silence of Mya.

Chapter 32

Steve and Kelly's house totally reflected their parenthood. Behind the cyclone fence were tricycles, a plastic playhouse, swing set, and assorted other toys. Also waiting behind the gate was a dog roughly the size of a Shetland pony covered in thick black hair.

Colton stopped on the sidewalk as Mya reached over the fence to wriggle the lock open. "Is it safe?" he asked.

Mya squeezed around the gate and held it while waiting for Colton to step inside. "Oh, Woodles is a sweetheart," she said as she leaned over the dog and gave her a hug. Colton gingerly made his way through the gate and stood stock still while Woodles happily licked his hands, and stuck her muzzle in his crotch which happened to be at nose-level.

Mya tugged at Woodles' collar. "Let's go tell them we're here," she said. The dog gleefully bounded toward the door, knocking over two of the several carved pumpkins lining the stairs.

Inside, they found Kelly leaned back in the recliner breastfeeding the baby. Colton blushed and turned his eyes away, pretending to survey the toy-strewn room while Mya headed straight to them.

"Take him," Kelly said as she pulled the baby away from her breast, and handed him to Mya. "He's just dinking instead of drinking."

When Colton heard the recliner snap forward, he dared to look back. Kelly was just finishing buttoning her shirt while Mya held the baby, gently swaying side to side.

"Steve had to make an emergency milk run. He should be back pretty soon. So maybe, Colton, you can hold Derek while we find

163

what Mya needs before the other four wake up from their naps," Kelly said as she motioned for Mya to hand him the baby.

Colton threw up his hands in immediate alarm. "I've never held a baby this little before. I'm not sure I know how to do it."

Kelly whipped the infant out of Mya's arms and plunked him in Colton's. "Then it will be good practice. Don't drop him and if he starts to cry, don't panic. He'll survive and so will you 'til we come back from the garage."

"Maybe you should know the dog licked my hands."

Kelly motioned for Mya to follow. "The dog's licked the baby."

Before he could continue his protest, Colton found himself standing alone in the middle of the room staring after them as they disappeared around the corner into the hall. He slowly lowered his head to look at the tiny face. An impossibly small hand was hovering near the mouth, while eyes were seemingly looking up at him. Then the baby yawned and closed his eyes.

Colton carefully moved one hand to touch the miniscule fingers. They closed around his. He studied the dusting of reddish hair and the moist little mouth sucking at an invisible breast; felt the barely perceptible weight on his arm. Unwittingly, a sense of protection rose in him. Babies were immensely fragile and defenseless.

The front door opened and Steve came through with a couple of gallon milk jugs in one hand and bag of groceries in the other. He hoisted the milk in Colton's direction as he headed towards the back of the house. "Just let me get this in the fridge."

He returned with the two women right behind him. Mya had a pile of material in her arms. Coming up to him, she gave the baby a sweet glance before smiling up at him. "I think you're a natural," she said. Kelly was rooting through items on an end table. "Steve, you know where my calculator went?" she asked.

"Kitchen," he said as he turned and head back the direction he had come from.

No one seemed the least bit interested in relieving Colton of his responsibility. Kelly totted up the cost of the fabric and Mya paid while Steve shuttled scattered toys into two large baskets. Colton slipped his hand back under the baby when he stirred and stretched in his arms.

Finally, Steve came over. "I'm gonna put him in the bassinet, Kel." He lifted the baby out of Colton's arms and headed out.

Kelly looked at Colton. "Just so you know you definitely have parenting potential."

Colton shook his head. "I'm so not ready for that discussion. It's a topic for later—much, much later."

Steve came back into the room. "So, Mya, can I ask a huge, ginormous, Woodles-sized favor? Could you please come with me Monday?"

Mya drew her eyebrows together in puzzlement. "Monday?"

"In some people's world, Monday is just Monday," Kelly said to her husband. To Mya, she said. "It's Halloween, and I don't want to take Derek out, but it will be harder than hell for Steve to wrangle all four kids by himself."

Her face lit up. "I would love to. We never get trick or treaters at the gallery."

"How about I pick you up at four? I'll drop her off when we're done, Colton. And, one more thing, the kids want you to wear a costume. I am going as Waldo."

*****

Halloween evening, there were no lights in the gallery when Colton pulled up. Mya must still be off helping Steve with the kids he thought. He vaguely wondered what costume she put together after Chaileen had emerged from the bathroom at quitting time dressed in her thigh high boots and an extremely revealing pirate outfit, which she flaunted in front of him.

"Going to a great Halloween party tonight, if you aren't doing anything," she said as she leaned her cleavage over his desk.

"Chaileen, I am in a relationship with someone."

"Doesn't mean you can't have a little fun on the side."

"I'm not into cheating. If I want to take up with someone new, I close down the old relationship first."

She straightened up and shrugged a bare shoulder. "Okay, but promise me one thing. When you are ready for some new action, you'll come see me first."

"Only if you promise me until it happens, you will drop any ideas of us being more than a couple of people who both happen to work for Jack Parker."

"Funny you should bring up Jack's name. He told me you were off-limits. So what's the deal? You his love-child or something? I mean as far as I know he doesn't have any kids or anything."

Colton looked at her as Mya's soft voice floated through his head. 'I don't exist… to him or anyone else who works there.'

"I'm just a guy who used to work on one of his construction crews."

Chaileen's expression was clearly skeptical. Colton kept his gaze level, although he wasn't sure who he was protecting… Mya or Jack.

*****

As soon as he entered the gallery, he was met by a very vocal Cinnamon. She followed Colton up to the bedroom and sat complaining on the dresser in the bathroom while he showered and changed.

Coming out of the bedroom, he wandered to Mya's worktable. There was a sheet of paper clipped to a calendar. It listed stores together with dates in November. He counted them and found she had scheduled nineteen business windows for painting over the next month. Next to the pile of material she had brought back from Steve and Kelly's was a stack of drawings with a purchase order clipped to it. Flipping through, he realized these were the sketches she had prepared for the music school which they apparently approved. Another list itemized cryptically named products she wanted to make to stock her online store for the holidays. And below in the gallery were the canvasses she was painting for the youth center. He shook his head at the volume of work she had lined up for herself. She was as driven in her own way as Jack.

Heading downstairs, Colton tried to figure out the riddle of Jack and Mya's relationship. He assumed Jack was behind Mya's contract with the youth center being reinstated while, at the same time, the man always verbally belittled her creativity by calling it 'finger painting'. Jack hadn't apparently had any direct contact with Mya in four years until their meet-up at the youth center, but he knew things about her current life like Colton's own involvement with her while the people who worked with and surrounded Jack daily apparently had no idea he even had a daughter.

And how the hell was he fitting into all of this? It seemed logical Jack had become interested in him because of his connection with Mya. Otherwise he would have been just another construction guy Jack wouldn't have had any reason to notice. Yet, when he was around Jack, no acknowledgement of the connection was ever made. It was like he was something Jack had somehow independently conjured up.

Checking the refrigerator, he realized they were probably going to have to go out if they wanted to eat tonight. Just then he heard the front door open. Mya appeared in the kitchen doorway.

A slow smile spread over his face as he checked her out. She was wearing her own jeans and tennis shoes, but she had on one of his tee-shirts under one of his Henleys. Her hair was tucked up in his baseball cap while his construction tool belt hung from her slender waist.

"Those aren't exactly regulation," he said, pointing to the plastic toy hammer, screwdriver, wrench, and drill fitted into the loops of the belt.

"I borrowed them from the kids. It is not a good thing to wear real hammers around small children who think they should be used on the nearest sibling. I did manage to con them out of a few treats," she said, holding up a small plastic pumpkin filled with candy.

"There's only one treat I want," Colton said as he moved in to kiss her. "The question is should I have it before dinner or after?"

"On Halloween, the best magic is close to midnight," she murmured against his mouth.

*****

It was verging on midnight when Colton found himself oddly wakeful. Mya lay asleep on his chest; her loose hair falling over his shoulder and the arm he held her with. The almost full moon, partially visible through the skylight, washed the bed in light, weaving its way through her hair and gilding her bare arm resting across his belly. A faint unease drifted through his body and nibbled at his mind. Maybe it was just the resonance of a day given to celebrating both the dead and the grotesque, or, more likely, the fact he was in the process of changing his life radically, a prospect carrying both anticipation and reluctance. Regardless, he was nagged with the sensation something was riding in the air, and it didn't feel good.

Chapter 33

Because it had been later than usual before he had fallen asleep, Colton didn't awaken until his alarm went off at 6:30 a.m. Mya was already out of the bed although Cinnamon was still curled behind his knees.

He dressed, and took a moment to pull the bed clothes into place before heading to collect his jean jacket. The weatherproof coat and boots he had bought Mya were missing as was her window painting tote.

Coming downstairs Colton saw the sky was just beginning to lighten. She was apparently already out the door. He filled his travel mug at the Keurig and tucked the tiny illustration she had left him into his pocket. For some reason today, he wanted a bit of her physically with him.

When he arrived at the office, he was surprised to find the door still locked. Colton let himself in, noting Chaileen wasn't there yet.

Reviewing the clipboard with the day's work, he just finished penciling out the order of his calls when the door opened and Jack came through. Colton looked at him questioningly.

"Wanted to catch you before you headed out, and, by the way, Chaileen called in sick today. It's either too much partying last night or she has some guy in the sack she isn't through with yet. Speaking of which, she giving you any problems in that direction?"

Colton shook his head.

"Good. She's a decent worker even if she is a slut. She just needs to keep her hands to herself on the clock. I don't pay her to play patty-cake."

169

The statement sounded harsh to Colton, but it answered a question. It was neither Mya nor him Jack was protecting. It was his wallet.

Jack pulled a large envelope out from under his arm and dropped it on the desk. "Here's all the information you need to start the property manager program next week. Classes are Monday, Tuesday, and Thursday from seven to nine p.m. You're on the clock the whole time. Be sure you wind up your regular work here at six so you have time to grab a bite to eat and get over to the school."

Colton eyed the package with uncertainty.

Jack sat on the corner of the desk. "I'm guessing you might be having some second thoughts about tackling a field that is pretty much virgin turf for you."

"Not exactly second thoughts, but definitely not confident in being able to hack it."

"Thought so. So here's what we're going to do. You and I will meet Wednesday and Friday after hours and go over what you covered in class and how it fits into real world property management. You'll be essentially getting a double education so when you pass your license test, you will be ready to move into to your new position."

Colton looked at him. "You do know I have a life outside of work."

"Mya? She'll suck it up. She knows how to do that. Besides, when you're done, you'll be bringing home some serious change. Make life easier for her."

"I don't contribute to the bills, remember? Your rules, I think."

"Well, then you'll be making some good bank for you."

"And that helps her how?"

"Don't worry so much. For the couple of months it's going to take, it won't kill her."

*****

Colton was stretched out on the bed, reading through the material in the packet Jack had given him when Mya came in with an irritated expression. She flung herself down on her back with a growl, crossing her arms over her chest, and staring hostilely at the skylight.

Colton reached to move some of papers to the other side of the bed. "Okay, what did I do?"

She tilted her head in his direction. "Not you. My stupid sewing machine. It's pretty old and the tension won't stay consistent any more on my quilt sandwiches."

"Do you want me to get you a new one?"

She sat up startled. "Absolutely not. I'm just bitching. I can quilt by hand. It just takes a lot longer. My plate is pretty full right now and I was trying to save some time. I'll survive until I see if I can afford one at the end-of-year sales."

Changing the subject, she gestured to the papers strewn across the bed. "What's all this?"

"This is the information on the class I'm starting next week. Your dad dropped it off today for me to look over." He paused. "Baby, this is going to demand a lot of time. The class is three days a week from seven p.m. to nine p.m. and then your dad wants to meet on the other two days for a similar amount of time to make sure I get what it is I'm supposed to get out of the class and to give me," he hooked his fingers in the air, "real world" training. I won't be getting home until after nine thirty five days a week from next week until almost the end of January."

Mya looked across at him, her heart beating a little faster. Her dad's takeover was starting. "Cinnamon and I will just have to fend for ourselves. Right, Cin?" Cinnamon was curled up on a smaller white envelope which had been among the papers. Hearing her name, the cat lifted her head, and stood up. She stretched before walking over Colton to settle herself in Mya's lap.

"See, she's good with it. We both just want you to do what you have to do to have what it is you want."

"You know the thought of leaving you two alone for so long without supervision is a little scary."

Mya rubbed her nose on the top of Cinnamon's head. "I won't tell if you don't, girl. What he doesn't know won't hurt him."

Colton began to gather up the papers. He picked up the envelope Cinnamon had been lying on, and stared at it a moment before opening it. He pulled out what looked like an invitation.

"Ahhh. Dad's annual Christmas party slash golf event for all Parker employees," Mya said. "Three days of sand, surf, golf, and fun in the rain at the Oregon coast which he always schedules right before Christmas so it can screw up most people's holiday preparations."

"Well, there is no point in me going. I've only been working for him a couple of weeks."

"My guess is you aren't going to have any choice since Dad is grooming you to be his right hand man."

"He doesn't own me, you know."

She gave a faint smile. Actually, yeah, he will, she thought as a sinking feeling took possession of her stomach. Now that it was beginning, she wondered how long it would be before her dad dominated Colton's every thought and action.

Chapter 34

The first week of the new schedule found Colton coming home exhausted nightly. A beer, a shower and he was ready to slide into bed. Mya would sit beside him quietly working on one or another of her hand stitched projects until very late; stopping now and then to lightly sweep her fingers through his thick hair or gently kiss his face, shoulder, chest as he slept. The situation didn't change the second week except Colton didn't get home until after eleven on Friday. When the weekend came, Mya was careful to give him space as he hunkered down at the little kitchen table with his course books and the additional materials provided by Jack.

Sunday evening, Colton closed everything, loading it in his old backpack. Setting it on the counter so he could grab it the next morning on his way out the door, he realized he had barely even acknowledged Mya. She had brought him coffee, beer, sandwiches she had walked some blocks to pick from the convenience store, and a Sellah totcho for dinner, but it might have been delivered by a ghost for all the interaction they had.

He went searching for her. She was upstairs, sitting in the glow of one of the task lights bent over fabric spread across her lap. He came up quietly behind her and squatted down. Nudging her braid aside, he kissed her neck. "Hey, I've missed you," he said.

She pushed her needle into the material before half turning toward him. "Welcome back," she smiled.

Colton slid her project off her lap and pulled her to her feet. Wrapping her in his arms, he kissed her thoroughly. "So, you got any plans for tonight, beautiful?"

173

"I'm not sure. I was hoping this hot guy I know might be up for something."

He slipped his arm under her legs and picked her up. "Totally."

Later, they lay facing each other. She was lightly tracing his face with her finger. When she pulled her hand away, he caught it in his, resting it on the pillow between them. "If this coming week wasn't a short one because of Thanksgiving, I'm not sure I would keep doing this," he said. "I hate having you pushed to the sidelines."

"You just worry about taking care of you. Dad can eat people alive. Don't let him. And speaking of Thanksgiving, we are invited to Duncan and Anita's for dinner if it is something you would want to do."

"What's my alternative?"

"I think Cinnamon has a can of turkey and giblets she might share with us."

Chapter 35

Duncan and Anita's home was a neatly maintained ranch-style in a neighborhood a couple of steps down from Quail Crest but still well above what Colton grew up in. They pulled up in front as the driveway was filled with Duncan's contractor van and the family SUV.

Climbing out of the vehicle, Mya carried a stuffed whale toy she had made the baby while Colton pulled out a six-pack of Hefeweizen. By the time they got to the door, it was already cracked open. Mya pushed through, calling "We're here." Anita's voice called back, "Kitchen."

When she dropped her bomber jacket on the corner of the sectional couch, Colton followed suit with his jean jacket before following Mya to the large kitchen. Duncan was just lifting the turkey out of the roasting pan and setting it on a large platter. Anita immediately claimed the roaster, carrying it back to the stove. The baby was in her high chair. She giggled and vigorously patted the tray when she saw them.

"Is that Hefe you have?" Duncan asked with a big smile as Colton raised it in his direction. "Other than your choice of women, you have some real taste there, man."

"Be nice," Anita said.

"She started it," Duncan replied, jerking his thumb in Mya's direction.

"Whatever," Mya said as she put the toy on Penny's tray. The little one squealed as she grabbed it and immediately began to chew on a flipper. "Can Aunt Mya borrow Daddy for a few minutes, sweetie?"

She looked back at Duncan and pointed to the patio door. "We need to talk."

"Whatever it is, I did not do it," Duncan said as he followed her out under the awning, sliding the door closed behind him.

"So, how is it going on your new job?" Anita asked as she whipped flour and water into the turkey drippings for gravy.

"It's okay. Jack's a pretty driven guy so he tends to think everyone else wants to spend all their waking moments on business."

"I'll be honest, Colton. Jack's not my favorite person. He was no kind of parent to Mya. Just let her fend for herself the best she could from the time she was practically a baby while he built his empire. I wonder sometimes if he has ever recognized the price she paid for him to be king of the mountain."

Colton shook his head unsmiling. "I doubt it because I'm not sure he even remembers he has a daughter most of the time."

Anita glanced out the kitchen window. "Oh, lord, how can those two be squabbling already?"

Colton followed her gaze. He saw Duncan standing with his fists on his hips while Mya's face was within inches of his, allowing for the difference in their height, with her arms folded tightly across her chest.

Anita glanced at the clock. "They have four minutes to settle it or they are both going into time out while you and I enjoy the dinner." Looking back, Anita noted Colton keeping a watchful eye out the window.

"You can relax, Colton. They have done this since Mya had the audacity to impugn his first-grade manhood by sitting next to him on the school bus. I mean the nerve of it all, a girl sitting next to a guy. Why his reputation was ruined for life."

The patio door opened, and Duncan stepped back into the eating area of the kitchen. "You are the stubbornest human being God ever put breath in," Duncan groused.

"I don't know why we keep having to have this fight. You are never going to win so you should give it up in the first place," she answered.

Anita pointed the cooking whip she had been stirring the gravy with at them. "Knock it off, both of you, or you will start dinner by showing Penny exactly what a time-out is. Duncan, carve the turkey, please. Mya and Colton, we can start carrying things to the table."

Dinner passed in a haze of excellent food and good conversation. Colton began to understand Duncan and Mya displayed their deep affection for one another through their banter and verbal zings.

"So who's ready for pie?" Anita asked. She was met with a chorus of groans. "Okay, who's ready to help with the dishes?" There was another chorus of groans.

"No volunteers, huh? Well, I didn't want to, but you are leaving no choice. Time to bring out my delegating skills. Mya, you are in charge of Penny. She needs a clean diaper, jammies, and her bottle. Duncan and Colton can help me in the kitchen."

Duncan shook his head sadly at Colton. "Sorry, man, you are family now so there's no getting out of it."

In the kitchen, Mya pulled a bottle out of the refrigerator, and placed it in the bottle warmer before getting a wet paper towel to mop up Penny's little hands and face. Swooping the baby out of the high chair, she disappeared into the back of the house.

Returning with Penny outfitted in pale green pajamas, she held out her hand as the open front of the dishwasher was now between her and the bottle. "Please," she said to Colton, pointing. As soon as the bottle was in her hand, she headed toward the living room.

In between the clatter of dishes being rinsed and stacked in the dishwasher, they could hear Mya's sweet voice singing to the baby about mockingbirds that don't sing and diamonds that don't shine.

It was quiet by the time Anita rinsed the dishcloth and hung it over the faucet. Duncan handed Colton another beer before they all headed to the living room. There they found Mya curled against the pillow back of the couch with Penny tucked up against her; both of them sound asleep.

Duncan set his beer on the coffee table before carefully reaching in to slip the baby out of her arms. Mya stirred, pulling Penny in tighter.

"It's okay, sis, we're going to put her to bed." Mya nodded sleepily and released her grip.

Anita took the baby from Duncan, who retrieved his beer and sat down in his recliner. He watched Colton position himself before reaching over to carefully tug on Mya's arm. He pulled her down until her head rested on his leg. Grimacing when her hair clasp gouged him, Colton fumbled to undo it.

Anita reappeared with a penguin patterned receiving blanket. She tucked it around Mya's shoulders before handing Colton the beer he had set down. "She's burning the candle at both ends again, isn't she?"

Colton nodded with a sigh, "And probably the middle, too. Any ideas on how to get her to take better care of herself?"

"Short of physically sitting on her to slow her down, nope," Duncan said. "I thought maybe when you moved in with her, she would relax a little. Doesn't seem to be the case."

"It's like she believes if she accepts anything from me to help make it easier for her, she is breaking some kind of law or something. I haven't been able to convince her otherwise."

"I wish we had answers, but we don't." Duncan said, glancing at Anita. "She grew up like an abandoned puppy on our street, shuttling between our house, Nancy's house, and her empty house. As hard as my folks and Nancy's folks tried to make up for what Jack wasn't giving her, I don't think she has ever grasped the idea she has enough worth to actually matter to anyone."

"Something HE exploited to get to her," Anita added. "You know about that, don't you?"

Colton's expression confirmed his knowledge. "Funny, I was probably your typical poor kid who always assumed rich kids had it made in the shade." He looked down at Mya. "But she sure didn't."

"Not even close," Duncan replied.

Chapter 36

Colton carried the large platter of leftovers Anita had insisted they take with them into the gallery before returning to the truck to bring a grocery bag with bread, mayonnaise, kitty food and beer. He put things away while Mya broke a part of a turkey slice into small bits for an appreciative Cinnamon.

"So, baby, what is your schedule tomorrow? Any place you have to be?"

She shook her head. "I still have three windows to do but there is no way I am going to try to paint windows on Black Friday. I re-scheduled them to Monday. Why?"

He came over and unzipped her jacket, sliding his hands around her waist under it. "Because I don't have to work tomorrow or meet with your dad. And what I really want to do is just sleep in, make love to a beautiful woman, eat leftovers, and forget everything outside our door until Saturday when I have to get back into the books. After tomorrow, we don't get a break until Christmas."

"Ummm, 'beautiful woman' is kinda generic. You might need to clarify so the wrong woman doesn't end up in the bed."

He slid his hands down onto her bottom, pulling her firmly into him. "As far as I am concerned there is only one woman anywhere, any time."

"That answer just might earn you a preview of tomorrow's action."

Friday evolved in a sweet interlude from the relentless demands of their immediate days. Mid-morning, Colton prepared them a brunch of eggs, sausage, and toast. Mya ate the eggs and toast, ignoring the sausage after one bite.

179

"Something wrong with the sausage?" he asked as he pointed his fork at her plate.

She wrinkled her nose. "I think I am sucking in too many paint fumes from the canvasses. Sometimes things just don't taste very good."

After cleaning up the dishes, they retreated back to the bed. Mya brought a sketchbook and pencil. "Hey, I thought we agreed no work today?" Colton said

"This isn't work. This is just playing around," she said as she settled herself against the pillows.

Propping himself up beside her, he watched her pencil wander over the page like it was on the hunt for something, leaving an indecipherable trail of graphite. Circling, swooping, turning sharply, the lines collected over the top of one another. He looked at her face. It had a different look from when she spotted something in her mind and was off to capture it or when she was deeply focused on teasing out a vision. This look was open and curious, like a fascinated child wondering what was next. There was a glow about her even the grey clouds hanging above the skylight did not diminish.

Colton felt a surge of resentment at the time they were going to be deprived of over the next two months and behind it a sense of incoherence. Mya was the catalyst bringing him into Jack's purview and opening the opportunities he was now experiencing, but those opportunities were apparently not predicated on his maintaining an actual relationship with her. If he was to walk out of Mya's life today, he doubted it would make a difference to Jack. She'll suck it up.

Lost in his thoughts, Colton missed when Mya's hand quit moving and just rested on the page she had been drawing on. Glancing at her face, he saw she had fallen asleep. He carefully pulled the pencil out of her hand and the sketchbook from under it; reaching back to set them on his nightstand. He leaned down to drag the plush throw over them both, soon falling asleep beside her.

When he awoke, Mya's head was resting on his outstretched arm, but the rest of them were separated by a sleeping Cinnamon. There was a smile in her blue eyes. "We have a bed hog."

"Yeah. I have never figured out she grows big enough to take over the whole bed, but she manages."

"Kitty magic," she said. Almost as soon as the words were out of her mouth, her eyes quit focusing on Colton. Giving her a boost to sit up, he grabbed her sketchbook and pencil; thrusting them into her hands. He doubted she even felt the tender bite he gave her neck as she bent over the swiftly emerging drawing.

Padding barefoot downstairs in his sleep pants and tee-shirt, Colton made a cup of coffee. He thought about making a cup of tea for Mya, but knew it would be cold before she realized it was waiting for her. Instead, he busied himself fixing sandwiches from the turkey leftovers. The sound of the refrigerator door opening and cutlery being pulled out of the drawer drew Cinnamon to the kitchen where she wove her way around his feet, begging for bits.

When the sandwiches were ready, Colton slipped the loaded plate back into the refrigerator to protect them from his marauding cat. He headed upstairs to find Mya still sitting cross-legged on the bed staring at her sketchbook. Sitting beside her, he touched the book. "You might be able to trade this for a sandwich with the works... mayo, dressing, cranberry sauce, and, oh yeah, turkey."

Her eyes still held their spaced-out quality. "Am I hungry?" she asked distantly.

Pulling everything out of her hands, he leaned forward to kiss her. "Yes," he said.

The rest of the hours drifted by until they fell asleep wrapped in each other's arms post-lovemaking; bodies sated. In the night, Colton jerked awake. He lay in the darkness listening to Mya's soft breathing beside him. Staring up at the black framed by the skylight in the ceiling, he felt a residual echo of something which seemingly passed through him in his sleep. The faint trail it left was rapidly diminishing, but it felt like loss.

Chapter 37

The warm bubble which held them the day before dissipated in the cool reality of Saturday morning. With a regretful sigh, Colton plunged back into his coursework while Mya vanished into the myriad of projects she was working on. Within a day after the start of the new week, Colton again fell into going to bed almost as soon as he came through the door where he was watched over by Mya and Cinnamon. Stitching beside him, Mya keenly felt the disquiet their relationship rested on. It echoed her growing up when each day was a trek over slippery hours of uncertainty. To obviate her fears, she chose to hold only the hour before her within and expect nothing from the ones beyond it.

As November turned to December, Colton was only peripherally aware Mya was gradually disappearing from his days. The course was challenging enough, but Jack kept pushing him to absorb more than he felt he could hold in his brain at times. There was little left for him to give to her, even on the weekend when he spent hours struggling to find sticking places for all the information being shoved at him.

She gradually quit sitting with him as she either worked behind the wall dividing the upstairs or went back downstairs after he was settled. He seldom recognized when she slipped into bed. In fact, with her early rising and late retiring, there were nights he didn't even know if she had actually been in the bed.

Then he had to break the news to her, as she had accurately predicted, her dad was requiring him to attend the annual Parker Christmas Party event at the coast. "Not only do I have to attend, he wants me to go down a day early with him to help with whatever. I'm not even sure what it is he wants me there for."

"Dad hates being alone and you're good company. Besides, you will be great skank bait. So, instead of the twenty-first to the twenty-third, you will be gone from the twentieth?"

"Something like that," he said unhappily. "I really don't want to do this."

She lightly kissed his cheek. "Dad plans a ton of activities and spares no expense. Just relax and have fun. Consider it a much needed break you totally deserve."

"And while I'm off hanging with your dad, what are you and Cin going to be doing?"

"I'm going to finish the last canvas for the youth center. I have two windows wanting a New Year's theme now, and I'm still working on the music school wall-hangings. You know the usual."

Looking at her, he thought, 'Yeah, the usual. All work and no break for you.'

Mya combed her fingers through his hair. "You're beat. You need to be in bed."

As soon as he was under the covers and she had kissed his shoulder, she slipped downstairs to find her phone. She was not excited about being alone next week but it made it so much easier to pull off the Christmas present she had been planning for him since before Thanksgiving. She quickly sent a text confirming the arrangement to Duncan.

*****

Over the next several days, Mya worked deep into the night to finish the last canvas she owed the school. Finally, at midnight on Saturday, she had stroked on the last coat of protective sealer, set the grommets, and finished sewing the ends closed on the sand rail. She leaned back against the gallery wall, exhausted, to text Wally it was ready. He would be delivering her check for all the mural canvasses when he picked up this one. Since several of the businesses she had billed for window painting hadn't yet paid her, it was needed to buy the materials she and Duncan required.

Tuesday morning, Mya helped Colton pack the duffle he had bought with the new sweaters, slacks, and slip on shoes which were more appropriate for time at a resort than his usual tees and Henleys.

When he was ready, she inspected him. Colton looked polished and sophisticated, not at all like the scruffy construction worker she had fallen in love with. He was morphing into a different man… a man who was beginning to reflect her dad. The son she never was.

A strange, but acutely vulnerable, expression settled on her face for a moment when he leaned in to kiss her. "Are you alright?" he asked.

She forced a smile and nodded. "I just want you to have an amazing time. You so totally deserve it." Her voice sounded bright, but there was tentativeness in her kiss; like she was retreating again. She walked him outside.

Starting his truck, he watched her standing on the porch, her face melancholy while her hair rippled in the wind. "Hang in there, baby," he whispered. "Just a few more weeks and it will all be alright, I promise."

As soon as his truck pulled away from the curb, she went back inside. She headed to make a cup of tea while Cinnamon followed yowling. "I know. I hate when he leaves, too. But there is nothing we can do about it except fill up time until he comes back through the door.

"So, for me, today's plans include getting my financial picture in focus; cleaning out the storage area so Duncan can do his magic tomorrow, and finishing some Christmas presents. It is coming you know and, if you behave yourself, Santa just might bring you something."

She spent the morning catching up her business books, balancing her checkbook, and printing out reports to determine where she stood financially.

Cinnamon was on her worktable, choosing whatever paper Mya needed next as her place to sit. "Just want you to know, you aren't helping, and this is rather important if you want those cans of kitty food to keep coming," Mya said as she picked the cat up, depositing her on the plush throw in the bedroom.

She was pleased when she finished as she was in a slightly better financial condition than she had planned even factoring in the cost of Colton's present. She should be able to get through the January to March slump okay if nothing majorly unexpected showed up.

After filing everything, she went downstairs and opened the storage closet under the stairs. She pulled out Colton's TV, gaming console, games, and papers, along with the lawn chair Wally had left him. She then began to sort through the odds and ends stored on the shelves, shuffling them off to new locations.

She paused to look at Cinnamon, who was sitting on the stairs watching through the spindles, when she pulled out three very new bath towels. "Please explain to me why I put these here instead of upstairs where they belong?"

Mya circled around and climbed the stairs. In the bathroom, she opened the doors in the old chest to store the towels. Having followed her, Cinnamon now sat in the doorway. "Ummm," Mya said. "Somebody we both know and love has destroyed the organization system again."

Pulling out the bath towels, she refolded them in a neat stack; followed by the hand towels. She reached in to pull out the washcloths jammed in the back corner. As she did, she uncovered her box of tampons.

Staring at it, heat exploded in her chest followed by iciness in her blood. She remembered having her period the week before the opening party of the youth center, but she could not remember having a period in November and so far in December. She realized she had so completely blocked any idea of getting involved sexually with another man after Victor the idea of birth control had not entered her thoughts when she so unexpectedly found herself passionately engaging in love making with Colton.

She was shaking as she finished putting everything away. She made her way to her tiny business area and pulled the calendar propped between the wall and her computer out. Flipping back, she began to count weeks. Nine. It was nine weeks since her last period.

"Omigod, Mya, what have you done?" she whispered.

Blindly, she headed back downstairs to work mechanically on clearing the cupboard, thoughts erupting, colliding, exploding and slamming through her. Just before she finished, she found herself hyperventilating. She sat down abruptly, dropping her head between her pulled up knees. As the wooziness retreated, she scooted back to lean against the counter.

She stared at her hand she had unthinkingly placed on her lower abdomen. She knew there were many reasons why a period could go missing. She needed to get a pregnancy test before she assumed it was the reason.

She got up and headed upstairs, coming down in her boots, and weather proof anorak. The rain outside was just a light drizzle but she planned on walking the almost two miles to the drugstore as a means of clearing her head and burning off some of the electricity riding her nerves.

*****

The stick confirming her pregnancy was carefully wrapped up with the rest of the kit and hidden deep in the outside garbage can where it would be picked up tomorrow.

She sat in the center of the bed staring at nothing, the doll she was making for one of the Barrett girls lay ignored beside her. She had never felt as alone and scared as she did at this moment, and there was not a single person she dare turn to. Nobody must know, especially Colton. She had made this situation and she bore the responsibility of dealing with it.

Turning, Mya pulled Colton's pillow into her arms; hugging it tight against her body. She buried her nose in the fabric of the pillowcase, breathing in his smell. It sparked a connection in her brain. What lay within her uterus was him, as well as her. A cloud of confusion began to gather behind her decision to keep the pregnancy hidden. If she did not let him know about the baby, was she protecting him or denying him?

Chapter 38

"Okay, you got those numbers?" Duncan asked the next morning as he triggered his tape measure to snap back into its case. Mya nodded as she ripped a sheet out of one of her sketchbooks.

Standing up, he headed to the kitchen. "What do you got to eat around here?"

Mya heard the refrigerator open, followed by his roaming through the cupboards. Coming back into the room, he was shaking his head. "The cat eats better than you two."

"Actually, other than weekends, Colton doesn't eat here. He's gone too many hours now that he's taking the course."

"What? So you only eat on the weekends, too, or does the cat let you have her leftovers?"

"I'm fine. There's plenty."

"Of nothing. Get your coat, we're going to Home Depot, the gaming store, and the grocery store. Anita saw what wasn't in that kitchen you'd be catching all kinds of hell and you know it."

By late afternoon, the storage cupboard had been transformed into a gaming center for Colton, complete with a fully outfitted rocker gaming chair. Duncan set up Colton's system and tested it out.

"Do you think he is going to like it?" Mya asked anxiously.

"Oh, yeah. This is a sweet setup if I do say so myself," Duncan said as he seemingly sprayed the screen with blood obliterating some military type.

"Okay, that worries me," she said watching. "Are all games that gory?"

"Only the really fun ones."

189

"When you are done killing whatever they are, please make sure it is shut off properly. I have no clue about that stuff."

While Duncan was taking a few more shots before shutting the system down, Mya went upstairs and came back with an envelope.

"Here, see if I figured right."

Duncan shook his head. 'I am not taking it."

"Yes, you are. We had a deal."

"No, you had a deal."

"Duncan, you just spent six hours here helping me with wiring and the shelving so technically you were on the clock."

"Let's just say it is a Christmas present to you."

"We had that out years ago. We don't do presents, remember? Unless it is fudge. Fudge is okay."

"Where is Colton when I need him to back me up?" Duncan moaned, as she jammed the envelope in his jacket pocket.

Chapter 39

At the beach, Colton found himself sharing a suite with Jack. He was grateful the two bedrooms were separated by a good-size sitting area. He was pretty sure Jack was not intending to sleep alone.

The first night, Jack had him follow along as details were checked and confirmed. "Pay attention because you will most likely be in charge of putting this together next year."

The next day at brunch, Jack checked his watch. "They should begin to arrive any time now. So today is check-in and then we're hosting a cocktail party in the ballroom. Your job will be to keep the ladies happy."

"What?"

"You know flirt, dance with them, get them drinks. You don't have to sleep with anyone, unless, of course, you want to."

"Jack, what part of 'in a relationship' don't you get?"

"It's business. It doesn't mean anything."

Colton threw his napkin on the table and got up. "Yeah, actually it does," he said as he stalked out of the dining room.

In his room, Colton stripped out of his sweater and kicked off his shoes before throwing himself down on the bed, cramming the pillow behind his head. He was beginning to feel he had made a huge mistake in taking Jack up on his employment offer. He had signed on to do property management; not act as a holiday gigolo or Jack's 'skank bait'.

Looking at the ceiling, he focused his mind on Mya. He gradually became aware he had not made love to her since the day after Thanksgiving. He barely remembered even touching her at all in the last weeks. She had been a sweet shadow floating around the edges of each day without comment or complaint. Jack was right. Mya was able to suck it up.

The words Anita used popped into Colton's head, 'the price she paid for him to be king of the mountain.' Mya was now paying a similar price for him to stake out a bit of the same mountain. Colton sat up, swinging around to sit on the edge of the bed. Maybe he needed to get out now. He could always go back to construction. A knock on the door interrupted his thoughts. Colton got up and yanked it open.

Jack was standing there. "Mind?" he asked as he gestured his request for entry.

Colton stood back.

Jack walked to the window overlooking the ocean, and stared out of it. "You didn't finish your meal."

Colton reached for his wallet. He pulled out a twenty dollar bill and flipped on the dresser next to Jack. "This should cover it. I'm going to get the next transportation out of here and head back to the Valley. I'm not the guy you apparently thought I was."

"No, you're not." Jack glanced down at the money before looking at Colton. "You're more the guy I hoped you would be."

"What do you mean?"

"You are honest and you have scruples. And you're straight up with me. As far as tonight goes, the only thing I really want to have happen is for you to have an opportunity to meet some of the people you will eventually be dealing directly with."

Jack clearly read the younger man's ambivalence. "Look, Colton, it's only a few weeks more. You've already put a huge amount of effort to get this far. Don't blow it up now."

Colton looked at Jack for a few moments. "On one condition. When it is over, you convince Mya it is okay for me to contribute to our expenses."

"Do you want it in writing or will a handshake work?"

Colton held out his hand.

Chapter 40

Mya was surprised to find hours could pass without her thinking about being pregnant. Then, suddenly the realization would catch her unawares, startling her. She had been able to settle two things in her mind. She would not tell Colton, or anyone else, until after he had completed his course and taken his licensing test. He had worked too hard for her to screw with his thinking now. And she needed to be much more proactive in securing work and sales to be able to put enough money aside to eventually pay to see an obstetrician. She wondered how long she could put it off without causing harm to the baby. Anita and Kelly had started going right away, but they had health insurance.

*****

When the twenty-third dawned, a little bubble of excitement settled in Mya's midsection. Colton was due home today. Even though she had guesstimated he wouldn't be back until somewhere between five and six, she couldn't help listening for the sound of his truck throughout the day.

Early in the afternoon, Steve showed up to pick up the kids' presents. He handed over a large holiday plate of Christmas cookies, candies, and breads. "Kelly got a little carried away this year. I personally blame Derek since she tends to get on Pinterest every time he chows."

Mya helped herself to a truffle while she made a cup of tea to take with her upstairs. She had all the finishing work to complete on number five of the six music school wall hangings, and number six to start.

At seven, the bubble had all but disappeared. She actually had no way of knowing if Colton would be home tonight. He had ridden to the coast with her dad; a man given to whims which could have both he and Colton staying another night or even to Christmas Day. In Jack's world, holidays had never been about family. Instead they were public relations events and business networking opportunities. As she and Colton had never established a habit of communicating much when they were apart, she wasn't expecting a message from him.

At eight forty-five, Mya carried her long empty cup back to the kitchen. She put a cup of water in the microwave to heat while she cleaned and filled Cinnamon's food and water dishes. The cat sat in her chair, voicing her thoughts.

Retrieving her heated cup, she opened the cupboard and began search among her numerous boxes of tea. "Cin, it does absolutely no good to complain. He will come home when he does. And, do you have any idea why I can't find my mandarin orange?"

"Maybe because you are out, baby?" His voice spoke from the doorway.

She whirled and held her breath as she stared at him, her smile lighting up her face. Colton crossed the floor in a couple of long legged strides and gathered her in. As she wrapped her arms around his neck, holding on tightly, he felt her body tremble.

"Hey, you okay?" he asked.

"I am now," she whispered in his ear.

Leaning back in his arms, her eyebrows drew together as she stroked her fingers along his jaw. "You look beat."

"Yeah. Your dad wanted me up and available to the early birds who might need something and for the late night party animals, and pretty much everything in between. It made for some long days. Not much time for R & R."

*****

Having fantasized about making love to her all the way home, Colton stretched out in the bed to wait as Mya shut down the gallery for the night. He was asleep by the time she reached the bedroom. He awoke the Christmas Eve morning, alone in the bed and let down.

The day passed much as most of their days had passed since Colton began his coursework. Although he had fully planned to pay more attention to Mya, it didn't happen as he doubled down to absorb the material he missed while at the coast. She, again, disappeared into the background.

A couple of times when he noticed as she came or went, Colton caught Mya looking at him with an enigmatic look, almost like she was harboring a secret. He assumed it related to the red bow tying the two knobs handles of the storage cupboard together complete with a hand drawn 'gift tag' warning against any opening until December 25. Mya had explained it was the only way she could keep Cinnamon out of the present she had made for her.

By the time Colton quit for the day, he had a headache and stiff neck. Mya fed him, gave him a couple of ibuprofen, and had him lay down with a heated neck warmer. The lavender essential oil she had put on the warmer encompassed him, relieving his headache. He drifted into sleep on its soporific fragrance.

At ten thirty, Mya covered him up before going to wash her face and brush her teeth. In the closet, she changed into her sleep shorts and a well-worn oversized sweatshirt before quietly getting under the covers on her side of the bed. He rarely touched her anymore, let alone made love to her.

A deep ache weighed in the center of her chest as her long-entrenched feelings of having little value were exacerbated by Colton's apparent loss of interest. It took a long time for her to fall asleep and when she did, it was fitful.

The skylight was still dark when she woke up. After staring at it a while, she realized she was not going to go back to sleep. Mya slipped out of the bed and headed downstairs. The clock on the microwave said six oh four when she put her cup in to heat.

It was nearing seven when she heard him moving upstairs. She went to the coffee machine and set it up. Mya pushed the button when she heard him leave the bathroom and go into the closet. Her smile was just a wisp as she handed him his coffee as he came into the kitchen before stepping around him and scurrying upstairs.

Colton watched her disappear. He had already berated himself when he woke up and realized, once again, he wasn't even sure Mya had shared the bed with him. It had been Christmas Eve, their first together, and it ended up being no different than any other day they had spent recently. It was all work, coursework, Jack, and fatigue.

Maybe he should have just gone ahead and quit that day at the beach; not let Jack talk him into spending three more weeks so buried he might as well be a hermit instead of a man sharing the same bed as a beautiful woman.

He finished his first cup of coffee and was headed to make a second when he heard Mya come down the stairs. She was talking to Cinnamon, who was squalling at the top of her cat lungs as she followed behind.

"Okay, I get it. You've been a good kitty and it's time to hand over your Christmas present. Maybe your tall, dark, and handsome owner will do the honors of getting them out for you."

Colton came out of the kitchen, raising a quizzical eyebrow. Mya simply gestured toward the bow while Cinnamon sat by the cupboard doors staring up at him.

Crossing, he pulled the ribbon, untying the bow. Handing it off to Mya, he pulled the doors open. "Okay, you spoiled brat cat, let's see what ..." His voice trailed off as he began to assimilate what he was looking at.

"It's all put together and Duncan tested it. He and Wally are gamers, too," she said. "You work so hard, I wanted you to have a way to kick back and relax."

Colton was stunned into muteness.

She circled him and pulled out the gaming chair, positioning it behind him. "You're on your own from here. I know nothing about this stuff." She then retrieved a package which had been hidden behind the chair and put it down for Cinnamon. "You're on your own, too. You want it, you gotta get it out of there."

He swung around. "Mya..."

"Merry Christmas." She silenced him with a kiss before heading to the kitchen. She returned with a fresh cup of coffee for him and a cup of tea.

He was already cycling through the opening of a game when she set his cup down beside him. "We're invited to Nancy and Wally's for their annual Christmas Open House. It starts at one. Tons of good eats. But I totally understand if you would rather just stay here and kill a bunch of whatever those ugly things are instead. Tomorrow starts another long week for you."

"I would very much like to go. Let me know when it gets close to one. I tend to lose track of time while indulging my blood-thirsty tendencies."

She bent over and brushed his thick hair with her lips before heading upstairs. Setting her cup on her worktable, she pulled out the drawings she was working on for the kitty magic concept she had been struck with at Thanksgiving. It was one of those frustrating projects she couldn't quite get to jell. She wasn't bridging the gap between what she sensed it was and what she was producing. She planned on giving herself until the end of the year to see if she could make it work. If not, then she was going to let it go.

For a few minutes, the sound of some kind of ultimate destruction reverberated upstairs, then it went silent. She climbed down a few steps and peeked over the railing to see Colton had plugged head phones into the chair and was completely engaged in pushing buttons on the game controller.

Chapter 41

She went back to her sketches; tweaking some and reworking others. About ten, her cell phone signaled she had a message. Putting down her pencil, she reached for it, guessing it was one of her friends offering holiday greetings.

Opening it, she saw the text had been sent anonymously. The message was short. Happy Holidays! From Your Bed to Mine! Attached were two photographs. The first one showed Colton holding a blonde haired woman by the shoulders as he kissed her. By the sweater he was wearing, it had been taken at the coast. In the second, he was asleep on his stomach in a bed. Although the bedding strategically covered his butt, his bare back and legs clearly showed there was nothing between him and the sheets while a red lacy thong clung to the edge of the bed.

Mya felt like she had been gut punched. She couldn't get her breath. As she struggled to get enough air in to keep from passing out, her stomach heaved. Dropping the phone, she raced to the bathroom, just making the toilet in time to vomit. She retched until there was nothing left. Flushing the toilet, she sat for some minutes with her forehead resting on the cool porcelain.

Finally she got to her feet. After rinsing her mouth, she washed her face in cold water before brushing her teeth thoroughly and swishing mouthwash around to clear the sick taste from her mouth.

Her whole body engaged in some kind of spasmodic jerking as she made her way around the upstairs wall to huddle in the pale light of the window. She rested her cheek on her pulled up knees. Now she knew Colton's lack of interest in her was based on more than the course and her father. Every explanation he had offered in recent weeks took on a different meaning.

Who was she? One of her dad's skanks? Whoever she was, she obviously wanted to make sure Mya knew Colton was cheating with her. Notice had been served. He now belonged with someone else and any rights or privileges she might have assumed she had with him were revoked.

But why was he still here since there was someone else? Had they agreed it was better for him not to change up his living situation until he finished the program and sat for his licensing test?

Although she had never trusted the relationship would last, and had tried to insulate herself from that eventuality, she was devastated beyond what she could have believed possible now the end was here.

Drawing in deep gulps of air, she dug down inside herself trying to find enough space to hold the agony. She would not let them make her cry or allow them to witness her pain. Her hand crept down to cradle her lower abdomen. And he would never know he had a child.

Mya didn't how long she had sat before she pushed herself up to her feet. She badly wanted a hot cup of tea to offset the coldness which had settled around her heart, but she didn't trust herself to actually see him at the moment. Instead, she swallowed the cold dregs left in her cup. The time on the phone was eleven thirty. She had an hour to nail her emotions down so they did not betray her.

It was Colton who came upstairs in search of her. He found her sitting in the light of the window stitching. He reached down to her. "Hey, beautiful, time to get going."

She didn't look at him as she maneuvered in order to ignore his hand as she got up. He wasn't hers to touch anymore.

Pulling his own jacket off the clothes tree, Colton watched as she wordlessly pulled on her bomber jacket, and tucked her hair into the slouch beanie. Her face was set in the neutral expression she wore when she had been hurt. Her eyes when they scanned past him were dark with pain.

He touched her face. "What's wrong, baby?"

Not looking at him, she whispered "It is what it is," and stepped away.

He waited on the porch while she locked the door before following her to the truck, reaching past her to open the door. Colton was careful not to touch her as she crawled in. He watched her face as he turned over the ignition. Even as she quietly stared straight ahead, he could see she was struggling for breath as well. For some reason, Mya was in deep distress.

He pulled away from the curb and headed to Nancy and Wally's house, located not too far from Duncan's. Maybe Nancy would be able to figure out what was going on because, right this minute, Mya was scaring him.

As soon as he put the truck in park in front of the Bergstrom's house, she got out and headed to the door. He trailed along behind.

Inside the door, Mya stopped, closed her eyes, and began to draw in deep breaths in an attempt to steady the turbulence within her. Colton watched anxiously. Coming into the living room to greet them, Nancy witnessed it; shooting a questioning look to Colton. He answered with just a slight shake of his head.

When Mya opened her eyes and saw Nancy, she forced a smile on her face. "Merry Christmas!" she said as she went to hug her. Nancy clearly felt the tremor in Mya's body.

"Merry Christmas, sweetie. Everything is in the usual place including Duncan hovering over the buffet table," Nancy said as she gently urged Mya toward the back of the house. "Colton, I'll show you where the beer is kept."

Nancy stood still until Mya had disappeared, then pushed Colton in the direction of the kitchen. She motioned for him to follow her through a door into the laundry room which she shut firmly behind her. "What the hell happened?" she asked. "If you weren't standing in front of me, I would swear you had died. I've seen her bad over the years, but never like this."

"I have no idea," Colton said, his expression painfully baffled. "She seemed fine when she went upstairs this morning. Then she was like what you see when I went up to get her so we could head here. I didn't have a gift for her today because she needs to pick out the sewing machine I want to give her. Could that be it?"

"Mya doesn't expect gifts on Christmas from anyone so I doubt she even noticed and she certainly would not be upset. How about phone calls or text messages?"

Colton shook his head. "I don't know. I was gaming and had my headphones on. But Mya hardly gets either one of those, and when she does, it is always from somebody like you or Anita or Kelly. Nobody who would hurt her."

Nancy nodded. "Yeah, it was just a thought."

"What can I do? How can I get her to tell me what is going on so I can help her with whatever it is?"

"You're not going to get her to open up. God knows none of us have ever been able to get Mya to let us in when she needs us most. The best I can suggest is just touch her, hold her, physically let her know you are there for her."

His expression became even more miserable. "In her own way, she has pretty much let me know she doesn't want me touching her right now."

Nancy's head dropped back. "Oh, Mya, why do you always have to hide in the abyss where we can't reach you?" Lifting it, she looked at Colton. "She is not going to be able to do this forever. One of these days, she isn't going to be able to bury any more inside herself. And when that day comes, she is going to break wide open. It's not going to be pretty, but it just might save her."

Nancy got Colton a beer and led him to the family room, bright with holiday decorations. A warming fire burned while the Christmas tree twinkled. Inviting trays of food covered two tables.

As soon as they entered, every eye looked at Colton. It was obvious Mya's emotional state had been interpreted accurately by the attendees. Nancy made a simple statement. "We don't know as per friggin' usual."

He looked around. Mya was nowhere in sight.

Nancy touched his arm. "I'll find her."

She was in the front room sitting by the carved crèche set Nancy and Wally had brought back from their honeymoon in Italy.

Mya touched the tiny baby Jesus in the manger. Then she studied his mother, Mary, kneeling prayerfully beside her Son. She picked up the figurine, cradling it in her hand. Mary had also been an unwed mother rejected by the man she loved until the Big Guy scheduled a talk with Joseph. Mya didn't know why, but for some reason the thought was actually comforting; not that she expected Colton to have any divine revelations. It wouldn't matter anyway. Their time was done.

Putting the figure back, she got up and slipped back to the party.

Observing, Colton saw her friends handle the situation adroitly. They managed to get food and drink into her hands and into her. They included her without expecting reciprocal participation; just surrounding her with conversation and distraction. Wally and Duncan were doing the same thing for him; urging him to sample the buffet while discussing gaming, his new job, and his perceptions of Jack.

A couple of hours had passed when Nancy edged up to Colton and whispered. "You need to take her home. She's exhausted." Simultaneously, Duncan and Anita announced the meter on their babysitter was about to expire. A circle of hugs and holiday wishes flowed around the room.

The last thing before they departed, Duncan pulled a large tin out from under the Christmas tree and thrust it in Mya's hands. "Fudge. Fudge is okay, remember?" He was able to actually elicit a smile from her as he kissed her cheek.

In addition to the fudge, Nancy loaded an enormous platter with items from the buffet, wrapping it and handing it to Colton. "Here. Wally and I do not need all of these leftovers. Our waists suffer enough this time of year."

*****

Back at the gallery, Mya got out of the truck, and opened the gallery door. She left it ajar as Colton followed carrying the platter and the tin. She had disappeared upstairs when he entered, shoving the door shut with his foot.

Setting everything down in the kitchen, he headed upstairs. He stripped off his jean jacket, dropping it on her work table before going to the doorway of the bedroom. She wasn't there.

Circling the wall, he found her staring out the window, her arms wrapped tightly around her midsection. Coming up behind her, he lightly kissed her neck before grasping her upper arms, and pulling her back against him.

"Please don't cheat on her with me," Mya said as she wrenched out of his hands, pushing around him. Colton was stunned into stillness for a few seconds before going after her. "Cheat on who? What the hell are you talking about, Mya?"

She was leaning against the door jamb to the bedroom with her head bent. When he neared her, Mya dove deeper into the room. Colton reached out and caught her arm, swinging her around so she faced him. She struggled hard against his hold.

"Mya, stop. I don't want to hurt you," he said as he tried to grasp her other arm. Her writhing threw them both off balance. Colton lurched to get his body under hers as they fell against the bed and onto the floor. Rolling over, he pinned her; grabbing both of her hands and holding them. She continued to squirm.

"Mya, please stop," he said soothingly. "Just stop, baby."

In her anguish she wanted to keep fighting hard against him, but his words reminded her she was not alone in her body and she let herself go limp.

They were both breathing hard when he released his grip and raised his body off of hers. She lay motionless, her eyes focused on the ceiling.

"Mya, are you alright?"

She turned her head away from him.

He pushed up to his feet, staring down at her. She did not move or respond. His presence wasn't helping anything. Leaving the room, he spotted his jean jacket lying where he had tossed it. He dragged it off the work table to hang it up, crashing something to the floor. Looking down, he realized it was Mya's cell phone.

Scooping it up, he opened the screen to make sure he hadn't broken it. His hand tightened around the phone when a picture of him asleep appeared. He looked closer and saw the red thong arranged on the edge of the bed. Sweeping his finger across the screen, he saw someone had grabbed a picture of Chaileen ambushing him at the first night's cocktail party precisely when it looked like they were actually sharing a kiss. Lastly, he read the message.

He had been set up and Mya had received what appeared to be evidence of his infidelity. Somebody wanted to destroy his relationship, and may, in fact, have done just that.

He carried the phone to the bedroom and squatted beside her. "I'm not asking you to believe me because of these," he said as he held the phone out, "but I absolutely did not cheat while at the coast.

I did not sleep with anyone and when Chaileen tried the kiss bit, she got a pushed away, pretty hard actually because I was done with her."

He paused and stared across the bed; his expression one of someone bitterly blindsided. "But I guess these show you have every right to think the worst of me and kick me to the curb." His voice was a husky whisper. "Maybe you should." Standing up, he tossed the phone on the bed and left.

She continued to lie on the floor while his words worked through her brain, 'kick me to the curb'. They triggered a question. Why exactly would someone want her to know or at least try to make her think Colton was cheating?

She sat up. For exactly that reason—to upset, anger, hurt her enough so she would let Colton go for somebody else to get their hands on. But who? The image of the skank at the opening of the youth center flashed into her mind. Her dad always had skanks around; some of them even had enough smarts to work for him.

She got up and sat on the side of the bed. Picking up the phone she looked at the pictures again. Although, they still made her chest constrict, she forced herself to really examine them. Colton's expression was startled and wide-eyed, not amorous, when the blonde was laying her lips on him. And while it could be construed his hands were positioned to pull her in, they were also perfectly positioned to shove her away as he said he had done.

She clicked to the next. This one was harder to look at even though there was no one else pictured. It was a killing thought someone else may have had the pleasure of his body. Her eye moved around the picture. Then she noticed the sliver of bedspread beside him. He had apparently flipped it to the other side of the bed where, what could be seen of it, lay over the unused pillows. It was not how a bed would look if two people had engaged in physical relations.

She lowered her phone. Whoever set up and sent the pictures had accurately counted on her being too shocked and upset to recognize they may not represent what they were purported to.

She clicked to her messages, highlighting this one. She held her thumb over the options before pressing delete. They could not have what she was not willing to give up.

Chapter 42

Colton was standing outside on the porch watching the cold winter rain fall against a darkened sky. It was the time of year when daylight lasted a scant nine hours a day. She went out to him.

When he heard her, he did not turn, but, instead, braced himself. Her voice was soft behind him.

"Colton?" There was a slight hesitation. "If you're not part of my world, then I don't think it's a world I want to be in."

He whipped around. The look on her face was vulnerable. She closed her eyes. "I thought I was going to break into a million pieces because you maybe had found someone else." Pain shot across her face and straight into his heart.

He reached out, cupping his hand behind her neck, drawing her closer. His thumb lightly traced along her jaw. "Baby, as far as I am concerned there is only you in the world."

She went into his arms where he held her tightly while stroking her hair. She turned her face up and kissed his shoulder and throat. He answered with his mouth on hers. She uncoupled the kiss to murmur, "You haven't given me my Christmas present yet," as she simultaneously slid her hand down his chest and over the fly in his jeans.

Heat began to smolder in his eyes. "It's waiting for you to unwrap."

In the bedroom, he reached for the bottom edge of his sweater and started to pull it over his head when she stopped him. "Uh-uh. My present. I get to do the unwrapping."

She slowly pushed the sweater up as her mouth delicately kissed all the sensitive places from his belly to the hollow in his throat. She directed his hands and mouth where she wanted to be undressed,

207

touched; kissed. Slowly, they savored each other until Mya shifted into him, letting him know he was now in control of taking them to the place where consummation waited.

Maybe it was because weeks had passed since they last made love or because they had come so close to being driven apart, their lovemaking left a luminosity shimmering through their bodies as they drifted back down into a state of deep peacefulness. Curled around each other, they were drowsing when Cinnamon leaped up. She sat on Mya's hip as she began to itemize a number of complaints beginning with a lack of attention and ending with a lack of food. Although Colton tried to shush her away, it was not to be. He reluctantly climbed out of bed; emerging from the closet dressed in sleep pants and a sweatshirt. He dropped Mya's sweat pants and one of his Henleys on the bed as he leaned over to kiss her.

"Cin may be on to something. Food is sounding good. Come on, beautiful woman, I'll make you a cup of tea and we can chow on what Nancy sent home."

With a little assistance from Cinnamon, Colton and Mya made a good dent in the leftovers, and decent inroads in the fudge.

After they had eaten, Mya encouraged Colton to play one of his games while she watched. He selected a game where the bad guys simply vaporized rather than one of the others which graphically included a lot of blood. After he got situated in his chair, she laid down beside it and put her head in his lap. Again, Cinnamon perched on Mya's hip to apparently watch as well.

After about an hour, Colton realized, despite the sounds of war, Mya was dozing off. She awoke and sat up when he shut the game off. He leaned over and kissed her forehead, "I think it's time I tucked you two into bed," he said, pointing to Cinnamon who was yawning widely.

She caught the tail of his shirt. "You'll come, too?"

He put the chair and controller away after closing down the system; shutting the doors. "Somebody who lives here loves to chew on wires."

"I'm sorry. I was out of dental floss," she responded.

He pulled her to her feet. "And here I have been blaming Cin. Upstairs, both of you."

*****

When he arrived at work the next morning, he found a key lying on his desk. "What's this?" he asked.

"Just in case you needed a place to stay or something," Chaileen answered as she sauntered to his desk where she struck a come hither pose.

She was unprepared for the look of loathing that came over his face as something dark settled in his eyes. "I was pretty sure I could guess who was behind the message. You played a bullshit game that badly hurt someone I love yesterday. And, yeah, for a while I thought I was going to lose her. If I had, you would never have seen me again, guaranteed."

She wasn't sure if he meant he would have just moved on or if he meant something more final.

"You love her that much?" she whispered.

"Yeah, I love her that much."

"I hope she knows how lucky she is," she said as she picked the key up off his desk.

"I'm the lucky one," he said reaching for the work orders to begin another week.

Chapter 43

"So what are we going to do New Year's Eve? Do you want me to try to make some reservations somewhere?" Colton asked as he sat across from her at the kitchen table Monday evening with his after class beer. She sipped her tea. "I will be babysitting Penny while I am pretty sure you will be required to hang at the Parker's Premier Properties annual New Year's Eve party."

"Mya, I don't want to spend another holiday with your dad."

"I doubt it's optional. Dad always does the Christmas thing for his employees. He does New Year's for all the people he has done business with during the year which this year will include Wally and Nancy. Duncan is going to be DJing and you can be Anita's date. She loves dancing and you're good. She promised to take out any and all poachers for me."

"I don't get a say about where I am and who I want to be kissing at midnight?"

"The party starts at eight so it may be possible for you to sneak out before midnight, if you want to."

"Oh, I'll want to."

*****

After showering the next morning, she caught a glimpse of her profile in the mirror as she dried off. She was startled to see her normally flat abdomen was curving out. She ran her hands over the small rise of roundness. The little human was growing and, in its own silent way, demanding she recognize his or her existence.

211

Mommy… like a whisper from within the word popped into her head. 'I'm going to be a mommy," she thought. She had been ambivalent about her situation since she discovered her condition; dealing with it by pushing it out of her consciousness much of the time. But in this moment when she could actually see the reality of it, she came down on the side of understanding this was going to happen, and she was absolutely okay with it.

Despite the excitement rising in her, she was still determined to keep it a secret from Colton until he had finished getting his license. She wasn't sure how she was going to handle telling him. "Hi, my love, congratulations on getting your license, and, oh, by the way, you're going to be a daddy in …"

She realized she didn't even know when the baby was due. She finished dressing and went to dig out her calendar. July. The baby would be due about the middle of July. She wondered if she was going to be able to keep up with her window painting, and, maybe this year, she should make application for a booth at the flea market since she was going to need all the income she could muster.

She would have to come up with some additional lines to sell if she was going to do the flea market thing. She had a few months to develop and produce items to stock a booth. She grabbed a sketchbook as she headed downstairs to fix herself a cup of tea. Sitting at the table, she opened it, and, looking down into her lap, asked, "What would make you happy to see, little one?"

Later in the day, the question of how she was going to tell Colton floated back to the top of her thinking as she sat stitching on the final music school wall hanging. It wafted up on a small cloud of unease. She actually had no idea exactly how Colton would take it. The only talk they had ever had about children was regarding other peoples' like Kelly and Steve's brood, and Penny. She fully intended to make sure he understood she would shield him from anything he might find distasteful about a baby, and she wouldn't alter their current financial arrangement because of her pregnancy. Although she had no idea how she was going to manage it, she was still the one responsible for maintaining everything.

She just prayed he wouldn't be so unhappy about the situation he demanded she make a choice between him and her baby.

*****

New Year's Eve, they pulled up in front of Duncan and Anita's house. Inside, Penny crawled to Mya who scooped her up. She was wearing red overalls over a white turtleneck with ruffles on the neck. Two red barrettes were nestled in her black curls. Mya nuzzled her baby neck before Penny tucked her head under Mya's chin, placidly beginning to suck on two fingers. She gazed at Colton; her brown eyes serious. Suddenly she pulled her fingers out and gave him a happy smile revealing four little white teeth.

He held out his hand toward her, and she grabbed a finger, pulling it in the direction of her face.

"You'll be sorry if she gets your finger in her mouth. She's like a little piranha right now," Anita said as she came into the living room. Colton carefully extracted himself from Penny's baby grasp.

Anita was dressed in slim black slacks with a red and black sweater shot through with metallic threads. She was wearing red heels, sparkly red chandelier earrings, and had several tiny red stars clipped in her hair. She wrapped herself in a black pashmina shawl.

"I hope you two know how grateful I am to have a night which does not involve green beans on my blouse, lesson plans for the classroom, or a husband snoring in front of the football game."

Colton bent forward to kiss Mya. Penny puckered up her little mouth and leaned towards him. He gave her the kiss. "You have to share with Aunt Mya, okay?"

He held out his arm to Anita.

*****

Jack had chosen to rent the Caverns for his party. New Year decorations were on every table, with hundreds of balloons trapped in a net spread across much of the ceiling. A catering company was set up at the back of the room while a secondary non-alcoholic bar was on the wall opposite the regular bar.

There was already a smattering of early arrivals when Colton and Anita walked in. Duncan spotted them from the stage and pointed at a table near the front. Jack apparently had been watching for

Colton because he rolled up almost as soon as they were inside the door. "I want you to hang with me so I can introduce you to people," he said.

Anita placed herself in front of Colton. "This man is my date tonight, Jack, so while you may borrow him now and again, he must be returned within a reasonable time. And I will be watching the clock."

Jack kissed Anita on the cheek. "Since I am not fond of getting my knuckles whacked, I never argue with a school marm. It's a deal."

Colton guided them toward the table Duncan indicated. They were joined by Wally and Nancy. The minute Nancy sat down she focused on Colton. "Did you figure it out? Is she okay?"

He had the answer ready since Anita had asked the same thing the second they were out of Mya's earshot. "Yes, and yes. We're okay."

Nancy leaned back. "So I would love a glass of merlot, please."

"A wine spritzer for me," Anita said. "My first alcohol in well over a year."

The men headed toward the bar.

Anita was true to her word. Several times, she felt Jack had exceeded what was reasonable and showed up to drag Colton to the dance floor. And once, when a slightly drunk woman waylaid him on his return from the restroom, Anita quietly came up, took his arm, and told her, "He's already spoken for and predators will be shot on sight. Got it?" The look in her eyes sent the woman stumbling off to hunt for other prey.

Sitting with the group, Colton suddenly understood what Duncan had meant by the three women using one brain. Nancy was cool and cerebral; Anita was strong and gutsy; and Mya was warm and heart-centered. Together they perfectly meshed into a force he did not doubt could be quite formidable.

The time had passed so pleasantly in the company of people who were becoming dear to him, he was startled when Anita announced. "Eleven fifteen. You should have just enough time to make our house before midnight."

Colton stood up and kissed both Anita and Nancy on the cheek. He shook Wally's hand and, grabbing his jacket, stopped at the stage to reach up and give Duncan a bro bump before heading for the door.

At quarter to twelve, Jack appeared. 'Where's Colton? I want him to release the balloons."

Anita looked at him with a twinkle in her eye. "Colton is gone. You weren't the Parker he wanted to kiss at the stroke of midnight."

Chapter 44

*T*he new year began much as the old year ended with Colton trying to keep his head above water between his job, coursework, and Jack's training. Mya again stepped back into being a quiet shadow of support. She finished the last music school wall hanging and gratefully deposited the check.

She was ecstatic when a large church running a day care center contacted her about perhaps doing some wall art canvasses like she had done for the youth center. She set a meeting to look over their physical plant, take measurements, and discuss costs and designs with them the third week of the month.

Colton eagerly counted down the last of the classes. The fourth week of the month, he would have the last two classes plus a day of review and take the licensing test on Friday. That week, Jack also wanted him to be part of the process in interviewing his replacement since the new person would be under his direct supervision. The following week, he would be training his replacement and officially moving into his new position the second week of February.

His first words to Jack, after acing his licensing test were to remind him of his promise to talk with Mya about their financial situation. It bugged Colton severely knowing he had banked several thousands of dollars from the months he had lived with her while she was always searching for and hustling enough work to keep the gallery bills paid. He had done his part, now Jack needed to make good on his end.

Colton stopped and picked up a pizza on his way home. The relief of finishing everything left him feeling physically light. Com-

217

ing through the door, he hollered. "Hey, girls, come on down. I've brought dinner."

Mya appeared at the top of the steps, her expression a question. He answered with a huge smile. "It's over, baby, I passed."

She quickstepped down and threw her arms around his neck. "I knew you would."

He gently ground his pelvis into hers. "Hmmm, I am going to have loads of free time now so maybe you can help me figure out how I might fill it."

"Let me think on it," she answered. "I'm might be able to come up with an idea or two."

Cinnamon also answered from her place on top of the pizza box.

They were a quarter of the way through the pizza when a cell phone rang. Colton and Mya stared at each other blankly for a moment as the unfamiliar ring sounded again. "My work phone," Colton said as he turned and started digging in the pocket of his jean jacket which he had slung over the back of the chair.

"Parker's Premier Properties. Williams," he said. He listened before standing up. "I'm on my way."

Pulling his jean jacket from the chair, he slid his arms in. "That was your dad. The police notified him water is pouring out from under a door at the little mini mall on Taggert. He wants me to go get the service van and meet him there." He leaned over and kissed the top of her head. "I'll be back as soon as I can." Reaching over her shoulder, he snagged another piece of pizza before heading to his truck.

As soon as she heard the engine start up, Mya looked at Cinnamon who had jumped up into Colton's vacated chair. "Seriously, girl, do you believe this? He's had no calls since he started and tonight when he's finally all ours, he gets a call?"

It was after eleven when Colton was back at the gallery. He looked wiped out. "Apparently the water fitting on the ice making machine in the deli gave and blew water into the massage therapist's office which shares the wall. We used the shop vac to get up as much water as possible out of the rugs, but we're going to have to go back tomorrow to get everything fixed."

He got up at his usual time Saturday morning. When Mya came downstairs to make his coffee while he dressed, she noticed he had brought the service van home. She gave him his cup and a kiss.

"I'm hoping this won't take all day," he said as he headed out the door.

While much of her was annoyed and irritated their first free weekend since November was screwed up, a small part of her was breathing a sigh of relief. It provided her an excuse to put off telling Colton about the baby. Yet, she knew her burgeoning belly would soon announce her secret, not only to Colton, but to the world.

She settled herself at her work table to develop the designs she had discussed with the church for the day care center. By late afternoon, she found she was wriggling in her chair because the small ache in her back was becoming very annoying. She decided to walk over to the little convenience store and pick up sandwiches for dinner and work the kink out of her back at the same time.

Chapter 45

The repairs and clean-up at the mini mall consumed most of the weekend. Mya sighed heavily when Colton left early Monday morning to meet with the person who would be assuming his duties after he moved over to her dad's office.

She could count on one hand the days they had been able to just be together and focus on each other since November. Maybe it was because the almost continual ache in her back was not letting her sleep well, she found she was more emotional about his absences, or maybe it was the sense of insecurity she was adding to by putting off telling him about the coming baby.

By Thursday morning, the pain in her back was bordering on unbearable. For every few minutes she spent at her work table, she needed an almost equal amount of time walking and stretching trying to seek relief.

Mid-afternoon, a weird sensation encircled her abdomen. It felt like a belt being tightened and then loosened. Then without warning, the tightening induced strong cramping. Mya doubled over, holding her baby bump protectively. Closing her eyes she tried to breathe through it. Eventually, the pain ebbed and her belly relaxed.

Whatever was going on frightened her. She leaned against her work table gently stroking the small bulge under her sweatshirt. "Come on, little one, everything's going to be okay. Just calm down in there."

Maybe she should go for a walk. It had eased her backache when she had walked to the convenience store and back. She went to put on her shoes, and gathered her anorak off the coat tree.

She carefully locked the door. Heading to the stairs, another wave of cramping hit her. She hung onto the porch pillar struggling to breathe through it again. As soon as they subsided, she let herself back in the house.

She sat on the bottom step and pulled her cell phone from her pocket. She touched through to Colton's number, then hesitated. This was not the way she had wanted to tell him. She pushed it anyway and listened. She disconnected when it went directly to his voicemail. She scrolled back up her list of contacts and touched Nancy's number.

Nancy's crisp voice answered. "Hey, girl, what's happening?"

"Nancy? Please come. I need you. Please come now." There was fear and something else in Mya's soft voice Nancy couldn't immediately identify.

The call disconnected as soon as Nancy said. "We're on our way."

Setting her phone on a step, Mya huddled miserably against the wall, her arms wrapped over her mid-section. She closed her eyes and focused all her energy on willing her baby to be alright.

Mya opened her eyes when she heard feet pounding up the stairs and felt the cold waft of air from the door. Nancy squatted down in front of her, putting her hand on her arm. "Mya?"

Fear glistened in her blue eyes. "I think something's wrong with the baby," she whispered.

Nancy looked hard at her. "Baby? What baby?" Then, she twigged. "Mya, are you pregnant?"

"Yes."

"Omigod, sweetie, how far along are you?"

"Sixteen weeks."

"Who's your doctor?"

Mya shook her head. Suddenly, she turned into the wall, panting her way through another round of pain.

"Mya, are you bleeding?"

As the pain backed off, she shook her head. "No."

Nancy looked back at Wally who stood just inside the door. "I think we need to call an ambulance."

"We can get her to the hospital before the ambulance would even make it here," he said.

Nancy turned back to Mya. "You need to be seen by a doctor immediately." Her tone brooked no argument.

Nancy stood up; stepping back as Wally leaned down. "Put your arms around my neck, hun."

Wally easily lifted Mya and headed to the car. Pulling the door closed behind them, Nancy ran to open the back door on their SUV. Wally carefully set Mya in the seat pulling the seatbelt out and buckling her in.

Nancy hurried around to get in the back seat with her. She reached out and took Mya's hand.

"Did you call Colton?"

Mya's voice was hesitant. "He…he didn't answer. I think he is out with the new guy."

Nancy stared at her for a long minute. "Colton does know about the baby, doesn't he?"

Mya turned her head towards the window in answer.

"Of course he doesn't." Nancy shook her head.

"He was working so hard on getting his license, and everything; I didn't want him to be distracted," Mya said softly.

Wally and Nancy exchanged looks in the rearview mirror. As much as she loved Mya, she just wanted to throttle her sometimes. She was going to do real damage to herself one of these days trying to make sure she didn't inconvenience anyone else.

They rode quietly for some minutes when Mya spoke quietly as she cradled her abdomen. "Please, little one, be okay. Just be okay."

Nancy squeezed her hand.

*****

Ume Choshi, one of the emergency room nurses, came out with a wheelchair to collect Mya when Wally parked in the emergency vehicle area and rang the bell beside the door. Nancy followed them.

"I'll be in the waiting room," Wally called getting back into the vehicle to move it to the regular parking area.

Nancy helped Mya get out of her clothes and into a gown. A smiling woman doctor came in and introduced herself. "How's your mom, Nancy? It seems I never get to see her anymore since she went to med-surg."

Before she could answer, Mya rolled on her side as she doubled-up. The doctor and Nancy exchanged sober looks. Nancy leaned over Mya. "You're in good hands, sweetie. Ume will come get me after you're checked out, okay?"

Wally stood up when Nancy stepped into the waiting room. "The doctor is with her now." Her eyes abruptly filled with tears. Wally pulled her into a hug. "It's not fair. It's just not fair. She never hurts anyone or asks for anything. Why can't Mya ever catch a break?"

Almost an hour had passed when Ume came into the waiting room. She took the empty chair next to Nancy. "There is no heartbeat, Nancy. Mya's baby is dead. Her body is trying to miscarry. Dr. Renson is giving her a little medication to help things along. I think she could really use someone with her right now."

Nancy bit her lip and fought back fresh tears as she stood up. "Wally, could you call Duncan and Anita? They'll want to be here."

She followed Ume back to Mya's cubicle. Mya was lying quietly; her hand gripping the hospital sheet so hard her knuckles were white. Her face was set in its neutral expression. Only her eyes betrayed the depth of pain and grief in her shattered heart.

Nancy didn't say anything as she moved to the side of the bed and took Mya's hand. Periodically, Mya would roll slightly onto her side while her fingers closed down painfully on Nancy's. Finally, she whispered. "It's starting. I'm losing my baby."

Nancy lifted the edge of the sheet as a wash of fluid and blood began to spread over the absorbent pad under Mya's hips. "I'll get Ume."

Nancy stepped out from behind the sliding glass door and looked around. She spotted Ume several cubicles down. She strode swiftly in her direction. "Ume? Ume! Mya's miscarrying."

In the practiced way of emergency personnel, Ume handed off some information to another nurse and moved quickly in Nancy's direction. She stopped long enough at the desk to ask them to let Dr. Renson know she needed to return to the emergency room.

At the door to Mya's cubicle, Ume stopped Nancy. "I'll come get you when it's over."

Nancy went back to the waiting room. Duncan and Anita were sitting with Wally. All of them looked up as she approached. "She's miscarrying now."

Anita got up and hugged Nancy. They rocked back and forth in their grief for Mya's loss. Then Duncan spoke quietly from behind them. "Where's Colton? Shouldn't he be here?"

Nancy pulled away. "He doesn't know. I need to call him." Wally held out her phone.

She swiftly tapped through to his number, waiting as it rang. He picked up before it went to voicemail. "Hey, Nancy, what's going on?"

"Where are you?"

"I just left work. I'm heading home."

"Don't. You need to come to the hospital right now. It's… it's Mya."

"What's wrong with Mya? Is she hurt?" She could hear his voice get tight as panic sent it into a higher octave.

"We're in the emergency waiting room. I'll explain when you get here."

Duncan looked at Nancy as she disconnected. "The man's going to come apart before he gets here. Why didn't you just tell him there was a problem with the pregnancy?" he asked.

"How many of us knew Mya was pregnant before this afternoon? Yeah, Colton neither."

Watching for Colton, all four of them looked up every time someone approached the entrance. When Ume appeared, she motioned to Nancy. They all exchanged uncertain looks as Nancy got up and headed to her. The two women disappeared from view.

A moment later, Colton spun around the corner, sliding to a stop. It scared him more than Nancy's call to see most of the people who Mya considered family in the waiting room. Anita immediately got up and went to wrap her arms around his neck. Resting his hands lightly on her back, he asked hoarsely, "What is going on? Please, somebody tell me."

Anita let go, and taking his hand, led him to the chair beside Duncan. She squatted in front of him, her hands on his knees. "Mya was pregnant. She's here because she is miscarrying."

Colton reeled back. "Pregnant? Mya was expecting a baby?" He looked at Duncan and Wally before looking back at Anita. "I didn't know. She didn't tell me."

Duncan nodded. "She didn't tell anyone; not even the girls."

Holding out his hand, Colton helped Anita stand as he stood up. "Where is she? I need to see her. I need to be there for her."

Nancy came in carrying two hospital issue bags with Mya's clothes and shoes. The yellow anorak hung over her arm. "You can't, Colton. She's on her way to surgery." Everyone else came to their feet as well.

Her face crumpled for a moment. Wally stepped up and put his arm around her shoulders; Nancy leaned into him and cleared her throat, "Mya started to hemorrhage while miscarrying. They're taking her to do a D&C to stop the bleeding. Dr. Renson said she would meet us in the surgical waiting room upstairs afterwards."

Colton reached out and slowly slid the anorak off Nancy's arm. Anita and Nancy exchanged looks. Anita took the two bags from Nancy before motioning Duncan and Wally to follow her. "We'll be upstairs," she said quietly to Nancy as they left the room.

Colton dropped back into the chair. Clenching the coat tight in his hands, he rested his elbows on his thighs and his forehead on the fabric. "What did I do to her?"

Nancy sat beside him. "You love her and she loves you. And when two people love each other, the greatest intimacy they can share is through their bodies. What you did was create something out of that love; the baby was your love embodied." She paused. "Mya wanted the baby, Colton. She wanted the chance to be the mother she never had."

"Why didn't she tell me?"

"She was going to... after you had finished with your licensing process. She didn't want to add to your load. And, maybe, she was a little scared you would be upset with her for being careless enough to become pregnant."

He was silent, but Nancy could see the muscles in his jaw tightening.

"What will she need from me now?" he finally whispered.

"The baby died, Colton. While none of the rest of us knew, Mya has carried both the knowledge of and actual baby in her body. She will grieve and she may feel guilt, thinking maybe she did something that killed her baby."

Colton looked at her sharply.

"It is pretty common anytime a miscarriage occurs, especially after the first trimester. She will need every bit of love, reassurance, and compassion you are capable of. And she will, no doubt, try to hide everything deep inside, just as she has always done." She gave him a moment to consider her words before standing up. "Come on, we should get upstairs."

"Nancy, just for the record, she would have caught me off guard, but I would not have been upset."

Chapter 46

Upstairs the five of them were the only people in the waiting area. Although their wait was relatively short, time still crawled slowly. Finally, a short, stocky woman dressed in green scrubs came in and took a seat on the coffee table across from where they were arrayed.

"One of you named Colton?" she asked.

"Yes. I am."

"I'm guessing you were the father?"

Colton nodded.

"Thought so. She called for you just as we put her under."

Nancy and Anita recognized the doctor's words nearly broke Colton. Duncan reached over and gripped his arm.

"Anyway, the surgery went well. She will be in recovery for about thirty more minutes, then she'll be moved to a room. Since it is so late, I'm keeping her all night. What her blood values look like will determine whether she gets released in the morning or early afternoon.

"Physically, Mya is very fragile. When she goes home, I want her to rest as much as possible for the next several days. There is no restriction on what she eats. She may have some cramping for a few days. Ibuprofen should help." She looked at Colton directly. "No sex for at least two weeks after she quits spotting. I'm going to send her home with birth control. She absolutely should not get pregnant again for at least six months. I would be happier, given her physical state, if she waited a year. Any questions?

"One of the nurses will come and let you know when she is in a room and you can see her," she said as she got up to leave.

Almost forty minutes passed before a nurse came to let them know they could see Mya. Colton was immediately on his feet. Nancy and Anita exchanged looks; each silently asking the other if one of them should go with him. Anita shook her head and Nancy nodded in agreement.

Wally and Duncan looked at each other. Their wives obviously just had an entire conversation with nothing actually being said. It always weirded them out.

Nancy stood up and touched Colton's arm. "You go to her. The rest of us will go get something to eat, then come back to check on her. Okay?" She was pretty sure he didn't even hear her.

The nurse showed him to the room. Mya was behind a curtain separating the bed from the doorway. Her eyes were closed in a face so pale her lips were chalky. Her hair was a soft river of brown under her turned head. One arm was tethered to tubing snaking up to a couple of bags hanging from an IV pole. Her body looked slight under the bedclothes.

Colton gripped the side rails as he stared down at Mya while the nurse circled the bed to check the bags. Looking back, she gave him a smile. "Doctor has ordered mild sedatives for her so she'll probably sleep most of the night. It'll ease her through the worst of the post D&C cramping." Her face sobered. "I'm sorry for your loss," she added as she left.

Colton looked around and spotted a chair. He brought it to the bed before lowering the side rail. He slipped his arm under Mya's head, cradling it as he gripped her hand. "I'm here, baby. I'm here," he whispered. She stirred slightly, opening her eyes. They didn't focus on anything before they closed again, but her fingers tightened around his.

*****

Nancy came the next morning bearing a take-out carton containing bacon, scrambled eggs, and hash browns. She also carried a travel mug of coffee. She handed them to him. "How did she do?" she asked quietly.

Gratefully opening the Styrofoam lid, Colton picked up the plastic fork inside and dug in. "She slept pretty much throughout the night. There were a few minutes when she got fairly uncomfortable, but they were on top of it with medication. They kept her hazy all night so I'm not sure she knew I was actually here."

Nancy smiled. "She knew. She just wasn't able to let you know."

"Can I ask a huge favor? They are going to be letting her wake up this morning. I need to stock up on groceries and I have something else I need to take care of before I bring her home. Could you stay with her? I don't want her waking up with no one here."

"Not a problem. I was going to ask if you wanted to go grab a shower anyway."

"It will take me longer than a shower but then I won't have to do anything, except take care of Mya."

"Take as long as you need. I'll call once we have an idea of when they are going to release her."

Colton picked up the mug and leaned over to kiss Mya before striding out of the room. Nancy watched. He had the air of a man on a mission.

Chapter 47

Linda was already at her desk when he pushed into Jack's office suite. "Is he in?" Colton asked.

"Yes. Do you want me to let him know you're here?"

Colton passed right by her desk and opened the door to Jack's large office. The man was leaning over blueprints spread on a side table when Colton headed straight to his desk. Turning, Jack watched as Colton dropped a keyring, credit card, and cell phone on it.

"I'm done, Jack."

"Done? What the hell are you talking about? You are one day from taking over the office across from mine. You have busted ass to make that happen and now you come in and tell me 'you're done'?"

Colton turned to look out the window overlooking the parking lot. "I nearly lost Mya last night."

"You mean she was going to kick you out?"

Colton swung back. "No. She almost died."

Jack sucked in air sharply before charging across the floor and grabbing Colton by his upper arms. "Died? What happened? What did you do to her?"

Colton threw up his forearms and broke out of the bigger man's grip. "I got her pregnant."

Jack stopped. "Pregnant? You didn't tell me Mya was pregnant."

"I don't tell you anything about her if you recall. And I couldn't even if I had wanted to because I didn't know until... until she wasn't. She kept it from me because she didn't want to interfere with me getting that damned license." He paused. "She hemorrhaged after losing the baby yesterday. The doctor said she is very frail. She

233

can't live by your dictates and carry it all alone anymore. For the first time in her life, somebody needs to be there for her, and that somebody is me. Nothing else is more important now because I can't risk losing her to a..."

"Grave." Jack answered softly before crossing to the credenza behind his desk. Reaching behind a rendering of one of his office buildings, he pulled out a photo and handed to Colton. It showed a young woman holding a baby. The woman bore a striking resemblance to Mya.

"That was Mya's mother and her when she was four months old. It was the last picture I had of Abigail before I lost her. The only thing that kept me from putting myself in the ground beside her at the time was Mya."

"I don't have a Mya," Colton said as he handed the picture back and walked out the door.

*****

Colton dialed Nancy from the grocery store parking lot.

"She's pretty much awake right now. We're still waiting for Dr. Renson to makes rounds."

"Has she asked for me?"

"No. She hasn't said a word. Just stares out the window while keeping a hand on her stomach."

"I'm at the store. I'll be there as soon as I can."

Colton pulled out the list he had worked on during the night. Still, it took him almost forty-five minutes before he loaded the bags in the front seat of the truck and headed to the gallery.

He moved swiftly as he brought in and unloaded the groceries, fed Cinnamon, and hurried upstairs to grab a shower and change. He had just locked the door when his phone rang.

"We're on our way. Dr. Renson released her and she wanted to leave right away."

"I'm here. I'll wait for you."

Colton watched out the front window until he saw Nancy's SUV pull in ahead of his truck. He hurried to the passenger door and opened it. Mya ignored the hand he held out to her, slipping out of the seat and crossing to the porch. Colton and Nancy exchanged looks before she got out of the driver's side and circled to the side-walk.

She handed some papers to Colton. "These are the instructions for her care. Dr. Renson is putting her on the pill for birth control. I'll go fill her prescription so you can stay with her."

Colton reached for his wallet. Nancy held up her hand. "We can settle up later. You go on in. I'll be back in a bit."

Colton found Mya sitting upstairs around the wall in the light of the window. She had her arms wrapped around her legs and her forehead resting on her knees. Her tangled hair pooled on the floor around her.

Retrieving her brush and a hair tie from the bathroom, Colton sat behind her with his legs spread on either side. He brushed her hair until it flowed smooth. He then braided it. He might have been working on a doll for all the response he elicited. She neither moved nor spoke.

He had just put the brush back when he heard the front door open. Nancy was gone before he made it to the first floor. The bag from the drugstore was on the counter. In addition to the prescription, Nancy had purchased a box of sanitary pads and panty liners.

He made Mya a cup of tea, choosing chamomile and lavender to help calm her. Colton picked up the two packages and carried them upstairs, stopping to set them on the dresser cupboard in the bathroom before taking the tea to Mya.

He sat it down beside her, touching the side of her face. "Drink this, baby," he said. "Nancy brought pads for you. They're in the bathroom." She responded by turning her face away from him.

Although Colton tried to support her as she floated in pain and grief, she would have none of his ministrations. He quietly circled; leaving cups of fresh tea which she may or may not have sipped, so little would be gone when he came to replace them with a fresh one. She ignored his attempts at coaxing her to eat something as well as encouraging her to lie down and rest.

By early afternoon Colton's frustration had a tinge of anger flaring along the edges. Mya was keeping him locked out just as she had kept him locked out when she was carrying the baby. Yes, it was less than twenty-four hours since he had learned about it, but the baby had been his as well as hers. His was the seed that sparked life in her.

Abruptly, the anger guttered out and he felt emotionally fatigued. He fixed himself a cup of coffee and went out to the front porch. It was one of those false spring days that happen in February; a taste of warmer, mellower weather. Just enough of a tease to keep Oregonians hanging onto until the real thing finally arrived.

Colton looked at the still vacant house across the street. It was almost a full year since he had dashed across this street into this place where he had so unexpectedly lost his heart.

Her face rose in his memory with all the expressions he had come to read and know; her smile, laughter, frown, frustration, focus, even fear and worry. Everything except crying. He had never seen her cry in the whole of their time together.

Chapter 48

Upstairs, Mya put her hand out and touched the cup Colton had brought her. She wanted so desperately to have him help her bear the pain, but knew if she touched him; went into his arms, she would break and the tears come. And if they came, she didn't know if she would ever be able to stop them again.

A whiff of hospital smell in her clothes caused her stomach to turn. She pushed off the floor stiffly, putting her hand out to steady herself on the counter under her sewing machine. She closed her eyes, waiting for the light-headedness to pass as her blood pressure equalized. When she felt stable, Mya went to the bedroom and stripped out of the clothes. She changed into her boy shorts and a tank top. As she put the pads and liners away, she saw her box of tampons. Immediately, her body reacted as it had the day she realized she might be pregnant. The past moment and the current one drenched in loss collided and she could not get enough air into her lungs.

Mya went to open the bedroom window, leaning against the frame. The earlier sun had disappeared behind a small seasonal squall. She welcomed the feel of the cold raindrops slapping her face and upper body; drawing her briefly out of her head.

"Mya!"

Colton swiftly crossed the room and pulled her into the circle of his arm as he reached out to shut the window before fully closing the circle with his other arm. There was something insubstantial about her as she leaned against him.

Mya braced her hands on his chest, trying not to give into his touch, smell, feel. Cracks began to form in her emotional wall. Her

237

hands clenched, gripping the material in Colton's Henley tightly as she fought to shut out the pain slamming against her heart. As her emotional wall began to break apart, she pushed hard against him, forcing her way out of his arms. She fled across the room and into the bathroom, slamming the door.

Colton followed. Putting his hands on either side, he put his ear against the door and listened. A soft mewling could be heard; a sound rising out of the deepest place of pain and loss. Mya was crying.

He called her name softly as he reached to turn the door knob. Immediately, he heard her attempt to stifle herself. Letting go, he leaned his forehead against the door. He recognized if he followed his urge to push in and hold her, she would do her best to mash everything back down.

"It's not going to be pretty, but it just might save her." Nancy's words repeated themselves in his memory. He waited, silently begging her to let it out—make room for healing. Then with a choking sound, she gave vent to all the pain she had buried.

The sobs increased in intensity until sound waves of anguish were breaking over him. He leaned against the wall beside the door, sliding down to sit on his haunches. Interlocking his fingers over his head, he pressed his forearms against his ears to mute the pain pouring through the door.

Colton didn't know how much time passed before he heard only silence. Getting up, he quietly opened the door. Mya lay like a broken doll on the floor; her closed eyes red and swollen, her face blotchy, and nose running.

She opened her eyes when he pulled the bath towel she was clutching out of her hands; carefully lifting her to a sitting position, resting her back against the tub. He dug in the cupboard for a washcloth he moistened with warm water before sponging her face and neck. Her bare arms and shoulders were cold, and the front of her tank top wet from rain and tears. He tugged it over her head, then yanked his body-warmed Henley off, slipping it down over her nakedness.

He helped her to her feet before picking her up and carrying her to the bed. She rolled on her side facing him as he pulled the covers up. When Colton squatted down beside her, she reached out to touch his mouth with her fingers as emotional exhaustion dragged her into sleep. Colton let her sleep until mid-evening when he brought her a tray with food. She opened her eyes as he turned on the reading light.

"You need to eat something, baby."

She rolled on her back and shook her head as she threw her arm over her eyes.

Sitting on the side of the bed, Colton put his hand behind her neck and forced her upright as he maneuvered pillows to support her. Spreading paper towels under her chin, he picked up a bowl of chicken noodle soup and began to spoon the broth into her.

Although the first few bites were swallowed reluctantly, she was eagerly consuming it by the end. She laid back. "I had no idea I was hungry."

He kissed her forehead. "You often don't. Now, work on this," he said as he put a plate bearing a toasted bagel with peanut butter and honey in her lap, "while I make you some tea."

She was not in the bed when he returned. He was gratified to see the plate was empty. He picked up the tray and set the tea down. She was back when he returned with a beer.

"Everything okay?" he asked, glancing at the bathroom.

She nodded, her expression quiet.

He went into the closet, emerging in his sleep pants and a tee-shirt. "I know it's early, but I didn't get a lot of sleep last night."

She tilted her head. "It's funny. I don't exactly remember you being there, but I remember feeling you there. Does that make any sense?"

He sat down on the edge of the bed. "I just wish I could have been there for you the whole time; not just the end."

Scooching down in the bed, she turned her back on him. He felt her disengage.

He reached for her braid, letting it slid across his hand as a sense of discouragement engulfed him. "Baby, please learn to need me," he whispered.

After watching her unmoving form for a few min\utes, he head-ed downstairs to lock the doors and turn everything off. Cinnamon followed him back up. Although, she usually liked to sleep on one or the other of them or between them, she settled herself on the far corner of the bed as though sensing care was needed this night.

Colton turned off the reading lights and crawled in beside Mya. He placed his hand on her ribcage, and was asleep almost immediately. In the night, she sat up abruptly, with a sound somewhere between a sob and a cry. Instantly, Colton was also upright, reaching for her.

"Mya, what's wrong?"

She drew her knees up, pulling into herself. "I had a dream. Something was wrong and I was all alone. I couldn't find anyone. There was nobody there and I was scared, so scared."

He wrapped his arms around her, pulling her tight to him, stroking her hair as she buried her head beneath his chin, clutching his tee-shirt. "You're not alone, baby. Not anymore."

Colton maintained his hold as he eased them back down onto the bed. "I'm right here whenever you need someone."

She was quiet for a few minutes. Then she spoke in a sleep slurred voice. "Promise?"

He tightened his arms around her. "Promise."

Chapter 49

Mya was in the shower the next morning and Colton was just finishing tying his shoes when he heard a sharp knock at the front door.

Coming down the stairs, he saw Jack's profile framed in the door window. He opened the door warily. Jack turned back. "Not much of a neighborhood, is it?" he said.

"It was what she could afford."

Jack nodded. "May I come in?" He was holding a vase filled with daffodils and two large envelopes in his hands. Inside, he set the daffodils on the counter by the door. "These were her mother's favorite flower. I ... I don't know what Mya likes."

"I think it's wilted daisies from the old gentleman down the block."

Jack nodded, with a half-smile. "That sounds like her." He set one of the envelopes on the counter beside the flowers. "I paid her hospital bill. She doesn't owe Trinity anything."

He caught Colton's stunned look "Hell, I got the money," he said a little defensively as he thrust the other envelope at the younger man.

Colton took it and, looking inside, saw the keys, credit card, and cell phone he had dropped on Jack's desk yesterday. Looking at Jack, he opened his mouth, but was silenced by Jack's upraised hand.

"I know what we talked about yesterday, and why. So here's the thing, you're on the time clock while you are taking care of my daughter until she is well and strong again, and I don't care whether it's a week, a month, or a year. When Mya is okay, then I want you come back to work for me."

"Nobody needs to pay me to take care of Mya. I choose to take care of her. I have enough stashed to carry us into summer," he said as he thrust the envelope back.

"Dad?"

Both men looked up the stairs as Mya descended. Colton realized with a start she was no longer just slender; she was thin... thin and pale. He glanced at Jack and saw Jack recognized it, too.

"I hadn't had an opportunity to see the gallery," Jack said smoothly, as he turned and walked into the exhibit area. When he came out he was holding his cell phone. He finished punching numbers in the calculator app.

"I want everything hanging in there," he said. "And according to the information on the wall, it totals $3,450."

"Dad, you've never had any use for my 'finger painting'. What's the deal now?"

"Your mother was a good artist. That's where you get it from. You're better. I have a lot of places art can hang in my properties. It will definitely enhance the ambiance which will help attract renters."

Jack caught the look that passed between Colton and Mya.

"And it won't hurt your reputation among the rich bitches in this town if they see your art in my properties. I think a Parker partnership might be beneficial to both of us."

He pulled out his checkbook and wrote a check out.

"It was $3,450, Dad, not $5,000," she said as she handed it back.

He tucked his checkbook back in his pocket. "It's a bribe so I get to see any new pieces first. I'll send someone over to pick them up Monday."

"Colton can bring them. He starts with you on Monday, right?"

"Not exactly, baby," Colton said.

"Colton is taking some well-deserved time off. He's going to start later."

Mya looked confused, "But..."

"And, Mya, I pay this man a hefty salary. I think it is time you started making him kick in his fair share of the expenses around here. Your mom and I shared everything, even when it was just a can of beans. It's a good way to live with someone you love."

He opened the door, pausing with one foot in and one foot out of the gallery. He looked back at his daughter. "I know I have been a missing-in-action, shitty dad your whole life. But, while I'm sorry it wasn't this time, I promise you when the time does come, I am going to be one helleva grandfather."

Mya looked at the check in her hand when the door closed behind him before looking at Colton. "Why does Dad care now what happens to me? He never did before. And how did he know..." She paused to draw a breath. "About the baby?"

Colton put his arm around her shoulders, steering her toward the kitchen. "I told him. Yesterday when I quit."

"You quit? Why did you do that?"

"Because being here for you was more important," he answered as he crossed to put a cup of water in the microwave. "What kind of tea would you like, baby?" he asked scanning the boxes in the cupboard.

"English Breakfast, please. And I can get my own tea."

He shook his head as he pulled a teabag out of the box. "No, you can't. The doctor said you needed to rest for a few days, which is exactly what you are going to do. You are to do nothing except, maybe, play with your art." He sat the cup in front of her and kissed the top of her head. "Let me take care of you... please."

She was quiet while Colton made breakfast. When he set their plates on the table, she looked up at him. "I'm confused. You said you quit, but Dad said you were taking a break and would come to work later."

Colton brought a paper towel, tucking it on her lap as he squatted down beside her. "I did quit because you need someone here until you are healed and feeling stronger. That's my job... the only job that really matters to me.

"I'm not your dad, Mya. My life does not revolve around work, although it probably felt that way while I was getting my license. My life is with you and Cinnamon. Managing property was just a way to earn money." He gave her a smile. "Apparently though, your Dad doesn't understand the concept of 'quit' so, yeah, I'll be going back when everything is good here."

She returned a small smile. "Dad can be really persistent when it comes to getting what he wants. And someone else is enjoying your breakfast."

Colton glanced over just as Cinnamon pawed a bit of scrambled egg off his plate.

*****

After breakfast, Mya carried a fresh cup of tea upstairs to her work table while Colton cleaned up the kitchen. Climbing up to check on her, he found her staring at a blank page in one of her sketch books.

She dropped her pencil with a tired sigh. "I just sold everything in my gallery, so it all needs to be restocked, and I can't find a single idea worth graphite in my head."

Colton circled the table to lightly massage her shoulders. "You have books full of ideas and lists everywhere of things you want to make. You're just not up to it right now. Give yourself time, baby."

"I am such a failure," she said softly. "I totally messed up on the most important creation I could ever have made." She dropped her head into her hands.

Swiveling her chair around, Colton pulled her hands away from her face, replacing them with his.

"No, it wasn't your fault. Something went wrong. Something you couldn't know or do anything about.

"Mya, Nancy told me how much you wanted the baby... to be the mother to it you never had. I get that. I would have loved the chance to be the dad that neither of us had."

She searched his face. "You're not angry at me because...because..."

He shook his head. "You didn't do anything wrong, except put me ahead of you. I'm a big boy, baby. I can handle stuff, tough or otherwise. But I can't handle things I don't know about.

"Your dad said something today that makes a lot of sense. We need to learn to share with each other; no matter what it is... even our last can of beans."

She tilted her head forward, resting it against his chest as she gave a small nod.

"Come on. I think you need to lie down for a while." He urged her from her chair, guiding her to the bed. He knelt on one knee to tug off her shoes.

"Could you stay with me for a little bit?" Mya asked.

Seeing the plea in her eyes, he kissed her forehead before circling the bed and climbing in to stretch out beside her. When he touched her, Mya turned into him, holding on as she had after her frightening dream.

Stroking her hair, he held her closely. Gradually her body relaxed until he recognized she was asleep. He eased out from under her, reaching to spread the throw over her.

Heading to her work table, he scribbled a message on the blank page of her sketchbook, adding a heart before carrying it to the bed and propping it against his pillow.

*****

Colton was just setting the table for lunch when he heard Mya come down the stairs. His heart beat a little faster as he waited for her.

She was holding the sketchbook tight against her chest when she came through the door. Stopping, she stared at him.

"Did you mean this?" she asked softly.

He moved to stand right in front of her. "More than anything."

Tilting the book away from her and looking down, she began to trace the words on it with her finger; her face set in its neutral expression. "I don't know how to be a wife."

"And I don't know exactly how to be a husband, but we'll figure it out. Just like we'll figure out how to be parents when the time comes." He put his hand under her chin, raising her face to him. "Will you trust... us?"

Looking into his eyes, she turned the sketch book around. Inside the heart was a single word.

Yes.

Acknowledgements

Love Imperfect was waiting for me one morning when I roused. Colton, Mya, and their story just needed to be plucked out of the ether and digitized. Once it existed in a tangible form, it required other eyes to determine its worthiness. Two fabulous beta readers stepped up to the plate: Kat B. Guerrero and Amanda Morgan were invaluable, for not only giving the story their thumbs up, but carefully picking their way through it to find necessary tweaks and corrections. Much thanks to these two word warriors!

Author Bio

L. Lee Shaw is the owner of the indie publishing house, Boho Books. In 2017, she debuted the award-winning young adult novel, *Aging Out*. She previously published *Blood Will Tell…* and *Monster Child*, and co-edited *Analekta*, an anthology of writing. Her middle grade chapter book, *Flunking Magic*, featuring a little witch who is very bad at spells, was released in 2018. The sequel, *Camp Dark Shudders*, is scheduled for release in 2022.

Learn more at www.bohobooks.com

L. LEE SHAW

AGING OUT

A NOVEL

✦ ✦ ✦

In helping a group of besieged elderly residents fight for their remaining future, three troubled teens might just find their own.